Laughing Raven Had Dashed out in Front, Knife Drawn . . .

Longarm bawled, "Get back here, you damned fool!" even as he trained his smoking muzzle to cover the crazy Crow. But the Contraries had by now noticed how far that special Winchester carried, and their circle widened a heap more as Laughing Raven made it unscathed to the fallen rider, hunkered down for just one grisly moment, and rose to shake a bloody scalp at them, yelling, "I count coup! See your brother's hair in my mind, you woman-hearts? What are you going to do about it?"

Also in the LONGARM series
from Jove

TABOR EVANS

LONGARM

AND THE INDIAN RAIDERS

JOVE BOOKS, NEW YORK

LONGARM AND THE INDIAN RAIDERS

A Jove Book/published by arrangement with
the author

PRINTING HISTORY
Jove edition/February 1989

ISBN: 0-515-09924-4

Jove books are published by The Berkley Publishing Group
200 Madison Avenue, New York, New York 10016.
The name "JOVE" and the "J" logo
are trademarks belonging to Jove Publications, Inc.

PRINTED IN THE UNITED STATES OF AMERICA

10 9 8 7 6 5 4 3 2 1

Chapter 1

An early autumn frost had crisped the cottonwood leaves along the Tongue River. But this day had dawned a good one on the High Plains of Wyoming Territory. So Little Wolf, the last untamed chief of Those Who Cut Fingers, known to outsiders as Cheyenne, sat bare to the waist on a medicine blanket spread just outside the entrance of his lodge, enjoying the warm sunlight on his skin even as he bared it lest the spirits mistake him for someone else.

This camping ground spread along the tree-sheltered banks of the clean-running water was a good one, good to spend the coming winter on. The Bighorn Mountains just to the west would rip the belly of the wolf winds and make the snow fall deep and gently on the lodges all about. There was plenty of winter browse for the ponies they still had left. The fall hunting had been good. Better than it had been since the terrible Cheyenne Autumn when Dull Knife and the others had been forced to surrender to the Americans, not because they had no hearts, but simply to keep the children from starving further. The women of Little Wolf's band had smoked much jerky and made many rolls of pemmican this fall. Nobody in the band would go hungry this winter. If only the band could survive until the friendly snow came deep, deep, to keep the Americans away at least a little while longer.

Down by the river's edge some children were skimming stones, and their laughter made the heart of Little Wolf want to cry tears of blood because it reminded him of an earlier time, the Shining Times, when a man had been free to laugh with children instead of worrying about them ever growing tall. The Cheyenne children at play knew Little Wolf was there. But they knew he was seeking a vision and didn't wish to tell them any stories right now. They were not afraid of the muscular middle-aged man seated on the baby-blue blanket with blue star-crosses painted on his naked chest. Cheyenne children were almost never punished by their parents, and the thought of a war chief showing anger to a child was unheard of. They simply loved and respected Little Wolf as much as he loved, and worried about, them.

The worried chief had just managed to put the playing little ones out of his mind when his low monotonous guidance chant was broken by Quails Drumming, riding in fast and sliding his pony to a halt close enough to lay dust on one corner of the pale blue blanket. As Little Wolf stared up impassively, the scout dismounted and hunkered down close to but not on the medicine blanket, saying, "Forgive me. I didn't mean to get dust on your blanket. I meant no insult to you or your dream spirits. Would you like to hear why I have ridden in so fast?"

Little Wolf nodded soberly and said, "I can see my son has a heavy heart. I think it would be a good idea if you told me what has you and your pony so lathered today."

Quails Drumming answered simply, "They have found us."

2

To which Little Wolf could only answer in a calmer tone than his own heart was speaking, "How many? From which direction?"

"One American, riding from the east, alone. He is not wearing the blue of the long knives. But he is armed with a short gun at his side and a long gun on his saddle. He is garbed in the color of tobacco. His hat and suit are both that color. He allows the face hair under his nose to grow. He has a silver star pinned to the front of his brown coat. I could have shot at him from cover. I was going to. But then I thought it might be a good idea to tell you about it before I lifted his hair."

Little Wolf nodded soberly and replied, "I think you would have made a wise leader in the Shining Times. Like the great Lakota sage, Buffalo Bull Who Waits, you saw the wisdom of a good fighter who likes to know all he can about an enemy before he kills him. One rider, alone, is no great danger to us and I would like to know how many of his friends might know we are here before we finish him off."

Pleased to be called wise, since in fact he'd merely been worried about making the wrong move, Quails Drumming tried not to grin like the boy he was as he asked, "Do you wish me to meet him with some other Crooked Lances and bring him to you all tied up?"

Little Wolf thought before he answered. "Since he seems to be riding in willingly, I think it might be better to simply let him. He may say more if he thinks we are tame dogs."

But then Little Wolf rose to gravely gather up his medicine blanket, saying, "I shall have a good buffalo robe spread for him to talk on. It would not be right to kill a man after he had even touched the blanket I share with the spirits."

Hence, twenty minutes later, as Deputy U.S. Marshal Custis Long rode into the Cheyenne camp on an Indiana Agency bay, nobody but the camp dogs and one bitty kid seemed to notice him until he reined in near the lodge where Little Wolf sat, alone, on a fine robe spread for the occasion. But as he dismounted, a young Cheyenne with a disturbing number of coup feathers in his hair sprang from nowhere to lead his mount, and Winchester, off to only the good Lord knew where.

The tall, tanned white man spoke a few words of his host's Algonquian dialect. But when he tried to howdy Little Wolf in the same the older man replied, in pretty good English, "Sit down, and maybe, if your words are good, you may live. I am called Little Wolf. I have never made my mark on the Great White Father's paper. Never. My people and me are not at war with you Americans this season. So why have you searched us out, why?"

The federal agent dropped to his knees on the edge of the buffalo robe and reached under his frock coat for two cheroots as he explained, "I ride for the law of my people, not the U.S. Cavalry. Neither the B.I.A. nor Army has anyone scouting for you. They already know where you are. As long as you and your band behave yourselves up here in this otherwise empty patch of prairie, the government has enough other things to worry about."

The older man scowled and snapped, "Hear me. I have never been afraid to behave any way I *wanted* to! I have lifted the hair of Pawnee, Crow, and Ute. I lifted much hair, much *American* hair, at the great fight on Greasy Grass Ridge near the Little Big Horn. I am Little Wolf. I have never been tamed."

His visitor smiled thinly and met the war chief's fer-

4

ociously flashing eyes as he replied, "Bullshit. I was detached from the Justice Department to scout for the U.S. Cav during the big scare after Little Big Horn. You boys shot your wad along with Custer in the summer of seventy-six. I'll allow you won that one grand battle if you'll allow we kicked the shit out of you in every firefight since. Once the Officers' Corps saw how dangerous it could get to play games with you in hopes of medals and promotions, we had your Lakota Confederacy scattered, whipped, and on the reservation rolls in less'n eighteen months."

The Indian looked as startled as a white lady who'd just seen a mouse as he gasped, "You call me a tame chief? You dare? In the middle of my camp, surrounded by my Dog Soldiers and Crooked Lances?"

The white man shrugged and replied, "I don't work for the B.I.A., so I reckon I can call you a renegade without having to do all that much about it. But you *did* make your mark on the paper when the army whipped you and the other chiefs fair and square. You agreed, in writing, to abide in peace on the playground set aside for you North Cheyenne near Fort Reno. Then you and Dull Knife busted your word and jumped the reserve in the fall of seventy-eight. We both know what happened to Dull Knife's band on the White River. We were both there. You and your people got away and, with winter coming on serious, nobody on my side figured you were worth the trouble of tracking down."

The war chief scowled even harder as he demanded, "Do you count coup on the White River fight? Are you proud of killing women and children?"

The white lawman shook his head soberly and explained, "I only helped the troops to track 'em that far across the snow. The troops did all the killing. There

5

wouldn't have *been* any killing if Dull Knife hadn't been such a damned old fool. But he and the few armed men he had left chose to make a fight of it, and every man there just did what he thought he had to do."

"It was a slaughter," Little Wolf almost sobbed. "Many women and children, many, were butchered like sheep by the long knives at White River. Can you deny that?"

"Yep. Half of Dull Knife's band was allowed to surrender, once the other half had been shot off. That's a better break than lambs get in a slaughterhouse, and some say it was more than a double renegade deserved. Dull Knife had been allowed to surrender twice before, and each time he'd reneged on the terms he'd agreed to. Considering the generous terms you boys offered Custer when the shoe was on the other foot, I'd say taking Dull Knife, again, alive, at White River, was generous as hell on our part. As to the women and children who might have wound up dead in the snow, it was Dull Knife's notion to lead a ragged-ass band of dismounted dependents into a winter fight with the U.S. Army. You, at least, had the sense to run like hell after breaking your word at least twice."

By this time, although the conversation still seemed to be private, other Cheyenne had drifted in to form a wide but solid circle around the two men growling on the buffalo robe. Little Wolf knew the brazen American had to know the situation he was in, unless he was blind as well as crazy. The war chief smiled like a coyote contemplating an unguarded newborn antelope fawn as he observed, "It is easy enough to say you spilled no blood at White River, surrounded by kinsmen of the people who died there."

The white man answered flatly, "I never came here to

tell you soothing bedtime stories. I say I count no coup at the White River because I wasn't called on to kill anyone there. But hear me. I count coup on many Cheyenne in good fights. I have killed my share of Lakota, Shoshone, Bannock, and— Oh, hell, let's just say I've never yet had to shoot a Papago or Havasupai. All the rest of you get to acting like assholes every now and again and, like I said, a man does what he thinks he ought to do for his own side."

Little Wolf suddenly relaxed and his smile seemed less forced as he said, "I know who you are, now. Nobody but the one they call Longarm would speak so straight to us at a time like this. They say you have always been a good enemy and . . . sometimes, a *friend* to us. Is it true you killed a wendigo that time the Blackfoot dream singers could not drive it away?"

His visitor smiled modestly and replied, "Some call me Longarm. I treat my friends and enemies as me and the law agree they ought to be treated. That story about me tracking down and taking out an evil spirit just ain't true. The so-called wendigo was an evil Spanish gent playing mean magic tricks for a land-grabbing crook of my complexion. If you don't want to smoke with me, do you mind if I light up my ownself? I smoke because I like to smoke. It ain't a ceremony where I come from."

Little Wolf nodded and said, "I am willing to smoke with the good enemy called Longarm."

So the tall deputy hauled out the same two cheroots and struck a waterproof match to light them both up as, in the middle distance, more than one Cheyenne relaxed his bowstring. Longarm knew that part was far from over, yet. But the Dog Soldiers hardly ever killed a man while he was actually smoking on the same robe with their chief.

Little Wolf inhaled a long drag that would have made many a white boy sick, and said, "This is good tobacco, good. I taste no cherry bark at all in this little cigar."

"There'd better not be any bark in these here smokes. They cost me three for a nickel. Would you like me to leave some for you when I ride out? I got plenty more in my saddlebags."

Little Wolf replied, conversationally enough, considering, "I am not ready to say whether you will be riding out, ever. I think I ought to hear why you tracked us down, first."

Longarm let his own smoke out with a grave nod to explain, "I didn't have to track you down. I sure wish you'd get it through your thick skull that everyone *knows* you and this band are here along the Tongue, damn it. Killing me won't change that in your favor. It might get you in trouble with the Great White Father, though."

"I have many young men. They have many guns," said Little Wolf with a brave shrug and perhaps an inward shudder. Then he asked, "If you are not scouting us for the long knives, why else might you be here? Are you tired of living? You do not look old or sick. But if you think this would be a good day to die—"

"I could kill myself just as good and no doubt a heap faster," Longarm cut in. "With all due respect to your growling manners, both the War and Interior departments have you and the other old chiefs of the scattered Lakota Confederacy on their books as peaceable, this fall. Yet they keep getting reports of one or more small war parties raising ned all across the rolling prairie to the east. Seeing as I have a rep for dealing with you boys, and no doubt seeing I work a heap cheaper than a cavalry patrol, I've been detailed to look into the matter.

I just rode from the Pine Ridge reserve, where I had a discussion of the situation with Tatanka-yatanka. He assured me none of *his* young men are on the warpath or even drunk enough to worry about. So I figured I'd pay this call on you and see what you might have to say about it, being you're sort of wild to begin with."

Little Wolf choked on his cheroot, coughed, and managed to ask, "Who told you the true name of Buffalo Bull Who Waits? I thought you people called him Sitting Bull."

Longarm nodded but said, "Tatanka-yatanka says it riles him to be called Sitting Bull, and I was brung up to be respectful of my elders. Do you want to discuss the complicated ways you pick names? The only names I'm really worried about go with the silly rascals who've been scaring settlers further out on the High Plains of late."

"Have they taken much hair?" asked Little Wolf wistfully.

Longarm chuckled despite himself and said, "Not yet, lucky for you as well as us. It only took one father and son, arrowed Cheyenne style, to set off the Sand Creek Massacre down Colorado way, and we wouldn't want a bad fight like that one again, would we?"

Little Wolf shrugged and said, "Black Kettle and his band were not ready for the long knives. They were at peace. They'd done nothing, nothing, and didn't know the Americans were cross with them until the fight was almost over. I am ready, ready, to take on anybody. If the long knives attack us, they will not get to just shoot women and children under an old weak chief. We will give them a fight their widows will long remember!"

Longarm blew smoke out both nostrils like a bull

9

beginning to be truly annoyed by fancy cape movements that didn't seem to mean all that much. He said, "Damn it, Little Wolf, have your young men been raiding or haven't they?"

The chief frowned and almost snapped, "I don't think so. I have not been consulted if they have. You must know my Dog Soldiers never ride far from camp. Their duty is to guard it. Most of my other young men belong to the Crooked Lance Lodge. Those who belong to that lodge are supposed to range free and wide to lift hair, ponies or women, of course. But they are not supposed to ride out without consulting me and the other elders. Such bad manners can cause a lot of trouble. How are we supposed to expect a counterattack if we are not told our young men have taken to the warpath?"

Longarm said, "Some say that might have happened along Sand Creek. *Some* fool Cheyenne put them blue-striped arrows in that white father and son. In other words, you're telling me and the Great White Father that you haven't ordered any raiding this fall but can't answer for *all* your young men?"

Little Wolf didn't cotton to that question, Longarm could see. So instead of answering directly, the wily war chief asked, "How do you know the raiders were Those Who Cut Fingers? If you asked Tatanka-yatanka about them, you must have thought they may have been La-kota, or Sioux, as you call them."

"I never call Lakota Sioux. I never call a gent of color a nigger or a Mex a greaser, either. I've yet to lay eyeball-one on any of the raiders we've been talking about. But the settlers they've been spooking keep de-scribing 'em as Indians and I got to start *some*-damned-where."

10

"Weren't they wearing paint?" asked Little Wolf in a disgusted tone.

"Feathers, too. But you know my kind ain't as up to date on face streaking as you and me. One old white gal recalled an apparent leader who rode his pony facing backwards, with his face painted solid black down one side and solid white down the other. But there's been no mention on the wire of Lakota red, Cheyenne blue, Arapaho green or, hell, Apache white medicine stripes. So for all we really know they could be from any nation, assuming they're not Hungarian or Dutch."

Little Wolf stared soberly through the cloud of smoke between them now as he muttered, "It is true. You do have a fair view of the troubles between our people. But why would Americans want to pretend to be members of the Contrary Lodge?"

Longarm said, "I can't say whether they're fake Indians or not, before I get a closer look at 'em. Such things have happened, starting with the Boston Tea Party. But to tell the truth, I've yet to catch a white man playing Indian just for fun. When Elder Lee massacred that wagon train at Mountain Meadows, dressed up as a Ute, his motive was plain and simple robbery, with maybe just a taste of religious hate thrown in. That wendigo case I worked on, more recent, was an attempt to rob the Blackfoot. These wild whatevers out on the Wyoming prairie haven't made a nickel at it, to date. What was that about a Contrary Lodge, just now?"

Little Wolf looked away as he answered gruffly, "Such things are not for women, children, or outsiders to know about."

Longarm snorted in disgust and insisted, "Come on, old son, I likely know as much about the Contrary Lodge as you do if you're really a member of the

Crooked Lance Lodge. Our Masons don't tell the Knights of Columbus all that much. I ain't at all interested in lodge secrets, red or white. I just want to find out who's been causing all this new trouble between our nations, and I do recall, now that I study on it, that warriors of the Contrary Lodge go in for acting bass-ackwards. How do you reckon a man could fight worth mention riding his pony facing the ass end of the same?"

Little Wolf said quietly, "I don't know. I am a Crooked Lance. I think I ought to talk to some of the other elders about this crazy riding against the Americans. If you know my people half as well as you say, you know how long it may take to give everyone a turn at speaking. It will be long after sundown, long, before we decide what we want to do about you and those riders you are after. By now your pony has been watered, fed, and rubbed down. I think we will put you in the lodge of Dancing Moon for now. She will feed you and see that you don't bother anyone else until we make up our minds about you."

Longarm started to protest that there was plenty of daylight left for riding. But Little Wolf said, "I have spoken." So that was that, for now.

Chapter 2

Things could have gone worse. Neither of the Dog Soldiers who marched Longarm to a spacious but sort of lonesome-looking lodge of sun-bleached hide set off from the others in a grove of cottonwoods thought to take his six-gun or even slap him around. They just ducked him inside, and one relayed the orders of Little Wolf to the lady of the house in their own singsong dialect.

Dancing Moon didn't like it much, judging from the way she hollered back. She was a pretty little thing, if one had an eye for high brown cheekbones and big sloe eyes. But her beauty was somewhat marred by the awful looks she shot at Longarm before she stormed out, fussing and cussing, to no doubt fuss at someone else. The Dog Soldiers smiled sheepishly at Longarm and then, not knowing what to say in a lingo they didn't savvy, they both ducked out again to let him work it out as best he could.

Despite the shade of the trees all about, the afternoon sun had conspired with the small smoky fire in the center of the circular lodge to heat things up a mite stuffy. Longarm took off his hat and coat, set them aside, and tried to make himself more at home by lounging on a buffalo robe with his vest propped against a backrest of deer antlers and buckskin thongs. He knew a gent was supposed to ask the permit of the lady of the house before he smoked. But since she wasn't there, might never come back, and had the whole interior blue with smoke to begin with, he lit a fresh cheroot and just hoped for the best. Getting out of here alive was shaping up to be about the best he could hope for. They'd told him at Pine Ridge that Little Wolf was still mighty wild. They hadn't told him this band was downright *crazy* wild, damn it.

A million years and another cheroot later, Dancing Moon came back. Her face was streaked with tears. She'd even blubbered down the front of her white deerskin dress. Longarm tried to say something neighborly in Algonquian. The Cheyenne gal snapped, "Oh, shut up," in passable English. When he did, with a sheepish smile, she added, "I am not cross with you about this. I only hate you, and all your kind, as one hates things like mad dogs and smallpox. Little Wolf was cruel, cruel, to make me take you in like this. He said it was because I dwelt alone and spoke your tongue. But hear me. If I speak English it is because they once stole me from my mother and made me go to a reservation school until I grew big enough to get away. I hated it there. They made us pray to your cruel spirits, and if we said one word in our own tongue the crazy old white woman in charge hit us with little sticks!"

Longarm nodded and said, "I had a teacher like that one time. I ran off to the war between the blue and gray as soon as I could, too. I can't say I enjoyed the war all that much, but school was just plain awful, and I *started out* talking English."

"I'm sure they were not allowed to beat you in school as they beat our little red behinds," she muttered, sitting on her heels as she rummaged through a pile of par-fleches, or rawhide boxes.

Longarm blew a nostalgic smoke ring and replied, "You're wrong. All teachers smack all pupils, now and again. It's the only way you can get kids to mind on a day old Man'tou made more for fishing than squinting at blackboards. I once got a swell licking at school and another when I got home for talking in class. I wasn't talking in your lingo. Some words are considered worth a good licking in my own."

The Indian girl smiled despite herself and said, "I know. Just before I ran away I wrote all the bad English words I knew on the blackboard. It made it easier for me to keep running, after it got dark and I got hungry. Well, Little Wolf says I must see to your comfort. I told him I can only try. If you do not like the way I cook you can go bother some other squaw."

Longarm raised an eyebrow at the term she'd used for herself. Then he remembered that while a Lakota gal would slap you for calling her a squaw, it was the ac-cepted term for a married-up gal among Algonquian speakers. He said, "How could you call yourself a squaw if you live alone, Dancing Moon?"

She began to mix parched corn and trading-post beans in an earthenware bowl, along with some runny deer fat, as she told him bleakly, "My man was killed by your people at White River, more than a winter ago. I don't want to talk about it. How is it you know of our Great Spirit, Man'tou? Why would he make good days for American boys to go fishing?"

Longarm said, "Your Algonquian cousins further east call him Manitou, if I'm pronouncing it right. My folk call him the Lord. I suspect anyone up there who makes things good has to be the same whatever. Don't you?"

She shoved her pot on the coals as she shook her head and answered, "No. Your Great Spirit is an American with a beard. He sleeps nailed to a cross to show how brave he is. Man'tou is a weaker spirit than your Lord. Sometimes I think Man'tou must have run away and left us after you people and your Lord moved into our hunting grounds. If he is still there, he never answers our dream singers anymore. They chant and chant and beat their drums all night before a battle and *still* you people beat us, beat us, beat us, as if *we* were the drums one beats to please the spirits! Hear me, my man had good medicine, good, at White River. He did everything right before the fight. I know this because I helped him paint himself for war. So where were our spirits when my man faced the long knives in all his glory? They killed him. The long knives killed him. Before he managed to even wound any of them!"

Longarm snuffed out his cheroot and gently told her, "That was not a good fight. Your people were on foot, in winter, with few weapons and hardly any ammunition at all. I'd be lying if I said I thought your man and the others fought with a lick of common sense. But they did fight, and they fought *bravely*. No man can do more than that, win or lose. You ought to be proud of him."

She answered simply, "I am. But we heard the Americans all laughed when they counted all our dead in the snow after they'd won so easily."

Longarm shook his head and said, "Not all of 'em. Just the dumb ones. All battles turn out easier for one side than they do the other. There'd be no point having 'em if both sides lost."

She didn't answer. She just knelt there, staring down into her pot for a time a white hostess might have thought downright rude. Longarm repressed his desire for another smoke on a growly stomach as the lodge filled with the scent of rib-sticking Cheyenne succotash. Speaking Algonquian, they even called it that. It was small wonder succotash was one of the few Indian dishes the whites had picked up on shortly after the *Mayflower* landed. So far he'd yet to meet up with an Indian nation that didn't have some version of corn and beans, albeit cooking the same in deer grease instead of water made for rib-sticking indeed.

Dancing Moon let her deep-fry succotash bubble some before she rummaged out a beat-up coffeepot, filled it from a water bag, and told him defensively that when and if she ever got near a trading post she meant to pick up some coffee, but that in the meantime she was serving herb tea. He said he didn't mind, and when she added that she had no flour to put in her tea, he said he minded even less. This was the simple truth. He'd never figured out why so many Indians put flour rather than sugar in their tea or coffee. But he knew it was surely an acquired taste.

Cooking over a bare handful of hot coals sure passed a heap of time. But it was still earlier than most white folk served supper when, at last, Dancing Moon swished her succotash one last time with a willow stick, raked both pots off the coals, and dropped a fistful of what looked like crumbled tobacco into the boiling water. She said, "I think it will be cool enough for you in a few heartbeats."

Longarm was a self-taught student of Plains Indian customs and didn't want to make his ungracious hostess any madder at him. But some customs just didn't feel comfortable to him and so, choosing his words carefully, he said, "It sure smells fine. But you've made way more than I could ever eat and drink alone."

She said simply, "I know. I made plenty, earlier than I do for myself alone, because I don't get to eat what's left until you are satisfied. I wish you'd start."

He repressed a smile, lest it be taken for mockery, and told her, "Men and women eat together, at the same time, where I come from. We don't have to tell your neighbors, and grease tastes a heap better if you eat it whilst it's still hot."

She hesitated. Then she crawled over to the low entrance and shut the door flap. There was still enough smoky daylight coming down through the smoke ears of her lodge to see what she was up to as she got out two horn spoons and a pair of tin cups before she crawled back to sit beside him, repressing a girlish giggle as she said, "I hope anyone passing will think we are only fooling around in here. I would never live it down if they thought I was eating like an American woman. But you were right about cold grease."

So, side by side and hip to hip, they dug in, cooling mouthfuls of piping-hot succotash with swigs of more tepid tea. At least she called it tea. It tasted more like boiled hay to Longarm at first. But once he got used to the surprise, he detected the scents if not the tastes of love grass, bearberry leaves and such and decided it wasn't so bad. Real tea or coffee might have left him more awake, and he was already more awake than a man who was likely stuck for many an hour in one place really needed to be.

After supper, as he smoked a cheroot and she took her supper wares down to the river to wash 'em with wet sand, Longarm glanced up more than once at the triangle of daylight high above. The sky was turning lavender now. The fall days were getting shorter and the sun would soon be down. It was during the tricky light

18

of a warm dusk, before they got the night fires really going, that a man had the best crack at slipping away discreetly. He wondered if the Cheyenne knew that. It was a dumb thing to wonder, when one considered how good Cheyenne were at stealing horses for fun and profit. The Dog Soldiers were likely hoping he'd make a try for his own mount, wherever in hell they had it right now. For while their code of hospitality forbade them fun and games with even an enemy guest, all bets were off if they caught someone messing with the pony line at *any* hour.

Dancing Moon took forever getting back, considering the time it could have taken anyone to swish a few items in a river. When she did pop back in she was flushed and laughing to herself. Then she saw him sitting there and asked, "Oh, are you still here? I thought you'd try to escape if I gave you enough time. The sun is down behind the mountains now. Were you waiting for it to get really dark?"

Longarm chuckled dryly and replied, "I'm still working on it. Is that why you just came in laughing, about an enemy who might be dumb enough to break the rules and wind up bald and fingerless?"

She put her things away, not looking at him as she said, "I don't think Little Wolf wants you to die. I was laughing because some of the other women were teasing me just now about having a man in my lodge at sundown. I turned the joke back on them by saying they were welcome to have you for the night in their own lodges. The maiden, Bird in Willows, screamed and covered her face with her skirts."

Longarm chuckled at the mental picture, knowing Cheyenne gals wore no underdrawers, and agreed, "That was mighty amusing, all right. Us monsters all

19

have hairy tails and stink of soap and water. What makes you think Little Wolf would rather have me just slip away, *alive,* I mean?"

Dancing Moon resumed her seat beside him near the bitty fire, even though supper was over, as she confided, "I think he feels caught between a buffalo bull and a bear, with no weapons. If he has you killed the great Tatanka-yatanka may be cross with us, and we really don't need the Lakota as enemies. We have more than enough enemies. You are one of them."

"I figured you meant we were the bear. Other Cheyenne, more anxious to keep fighting us, might call him woman-hearted if he gave enough help to matter to a lawman tracking bad Indians of any nation, right?"

She stared down into the ruby coals between them and the closed entrance flap as she replied quietly, "I heard some of the men talking about it when I went to the river. The raiders you are after sound like Contraries. So there is more to it than just telling one of your kind about young men simply out to count coup without the approval of their elders. Hear me, I am a woman of Those Who Cut Fingers. My father was a member of the Crooked Lance Lodge. My husband was a member of the Crooked Lance Lodge. I know nothing, nothing, of the secret rites they both took part in. The Contrary Lodge is older, older, with much medicine and many secrets. The old ones say the Contrary Lodge began in the Grandfather Times, before we had horses, or even lived out here on the sea of grass. The old ones say the vision of the Contraries was given to them in a lodge of birch bark by the Great Sweet Water, east of the sunrise."

She lowered her voice even more as she repressed a shudder and added, "Some say that even long ago, some feared the medicine of Man'tou was not strong enough, and so they sought the help of . . . Wendigo!"

Longarm whistled softly. They both knew that if Man'tou was about the same as the white man's Lord, Wendigo had to be the Devil. "I can see why the Contrary Lodge makes both your folk and mine sort of nervous. I thought they were just a clan that acted, well, *contrary,* doing everything sort of left-handed and backwards. Little Wolf tells me there ain't no such, ah, devil worship, going on in this band. Do you reckon he told me the truth?"

She turned her face to him, sloe eyes flashing in the ruby light, to snap, "Hear me! Little Wolf, like my father and my poor husband were, is a Crooked Lance. Men of that lodge never lie, never! I am very cross with you for even asking such a foolish question!"

He shrugged and said, "I ask a lot of questions, foolish or otherwise, because asking questions goes with my job. I ain't out to insult nobody just for fun. I'll take the word of a lady on the Crooked Lance sense of honor. I've heard as much from more'n one old army man. But I'm missing something, here. If Little Wolf never fibs, and if he says none of his boys belong to the Contrary cult—"

"You are foolish, foolish!" she cut in. "They say you try to understand us more than most of your kind do. But you do not really understand us at all. You just said yourself that a Contrary does everything he can *backwards,* the way no other man of our nation would. Those Who Cut Fingers take pride in always speaking with a straight tongue. As children we are all taught to deal honestly, even with enemies, and never steal anything but horses. That is the path of Man'tou, not *Wendigo,* you fool!"

21

He nodded in understanding and said, "In other words, anyone in your band who'd signed up with the Contrary Lodge would just naturally lie about it, even to his own chief, and poor Little Wolf, being used to even the kids admitting to any cherry trees missing in action, would have a tougher time than your average white man would at spotting a barefaced liar!"

She allowed he was learning, and seemed to move just a mite closer, covering a yawn with a delicate brown hand. That confused him more than it upset him. Indians running free smelled different but not really worse than his own kind. They made up for not having real soap or toilet water by bathing more often, at least in warm weather, than most white folk. He could tell her notion of French perfume was sagebrush smoke. But it stunk her up sort of wild and free, and the picture of her squatting naked over hot rocks and steaming herbs added a certain spice to her tawny flesh that couldn't be any worse than the whale puke they added to the most expensive perfume white gals fancied. But while he was tempted to wrap a casual arm around her, lest she fall backward through the thongs they were leaning against, he was still lawman enough to say, "Hold on. If you, Little Wolf, and your Man'tou agree fibbing is a serious sin, why would Little Wolf want to cover up for liars of any complexion?"

She yawned again and said, "It's *not* wrong for *Contraries* to lie. They shoot left-handed and ride into battle backwards as well. Doing things the way nobody else might do them is just the medicine they were given. We hate you Americans when you lie because you do everything else about right. You only lie so much to take advantage of us, see?"

He sighed and said, "Well, we do mount our ponies

from the left instead of the right, Indian style. And I know better than to argue with an unreconstructed Cheyenne about the small print on some of the treaties drawn up between an illiterate chief and a pencil-pushing lawyer who didn't understand the folk he was trying to make a deal with. My side ain't the only one to find the notion sort of confusing. I'm glad you set me straight on the confused loyalties of Little Wolf, though. What happens next?"

She shrugged, close enough now for him to feel it, and told him, "They are still talking about it, over at the lodge of Little Wolf. Some will say they are tired of fighting and that it might be a good idea to just send you on your way. Others, who may not have been in as many fights with the long knives, will argue that since you have found our camp, it would be foolish to let you go. No matter what they decide, in the end, Little Wolf won't let anyone kill you here in camp. That would be a bad thing. You will know when you ride out, in the morning. If those who want your hair win the hearts of the elders, they will attack you at least out of sight of camp. Nothing will happen to you before then, unless you leave this lodge. Would you like to fuck me, now?"

Longarm gulped and replied, "I didn't know the choice was mine. I understood you'd agreed to shelter me here for the night with considerable reluctance."

She nodded soberly and said, "You are my enemy for as long as I draw breath. Your kind killed my father at Greasy Grass and my man at White River. If I was a man, I would kill you, cut off your bow fingers, and count coup on you, no matter what Tatanka-yatanka says about you."

He sighed and said, "I wish you'd make up your mind, you pretty little thing. I read some fool place that love and hate are opposing sides of the same coin. But most gals ain't quite as blunt on the subject. I reckon it's on account they taught you English straight and simple. Our own gals hardly ever put things so plain, either way."

"I know. I asked the crazy teachers at that school why 'fuck' was a bad word, once I found out what it meant. They just washed my mouth out with soap until I learned not to ask them anything. I thought you had more sense than old women who never got to fuck. Don't you *like* to?"

He laughed despite himself and said, "More than I ought to, I sometimes fear. But you just said you'd like to kill me, didn't you?"

She nodded to say, "I am a woman. I am not supposed to count coup on enemies and even if I could, Little Wolf would be cross with me if I mistreated a guest. Hear me. I was told to treat you good. I have fed you as well as I could. Now it is my duty to please you with my body as good as I am able."

"Even hating my guts?" asked Longarm with a gentle smile.

"The pleasures of fighting and fucking have nothing to do with each other. You are big and strong and not bad looking. I have not had a man in many moons, and if they kill you in the morning you will never have another woman. I don't see what's so complicated about that."

She must have meant it. For the next thing he knew she'd peeled off her deerskin dress and spread herself out on the nearby hides and blankets, bold as brass and mighty nice to look at in the flickering ruby light of the dying fire. He didn't want her to remember him as a sissy, dead or alive, so he just hung up his six-gun,

24

shucked his boots and duds, and joined her in the same
condition of smoke-scented nudity.

He took her in his arms and started to kiss her. She
turned her face from his and murmured, "Don't treat me
like one of your silly American women. Just *do* it and
get it over with so I can get some sleep, you big
enemy!"

Now, as any man born of mortal woman knows,
there is no way short of a pail of ice water that can cool
a man's desire more than some snippy female spreading
her thighs and telling him to just get it over with. So
Dancing Moon came mighty close to remaining pure as
ever, tempting as she lay there with the soft light casting
the long shadows of her turgid nipples across her firm
brown breasts. But Longarm had met cruel-mouthed
women in the past, so he knew that no matter what they
might say at a time like this, it was a better than even-
money bet they'd get mad as hell if a man took 'em up
on it.

He didn't want her any madder at him than she already seemed to be, seeing he was stuck here for now
and that she had more than one knife among her cooking utensils. So, seeing she'd told him he could, he got
it up just enough to slip it sort of into her. Then, as it
felt how warm and wet she was down yonder, despite
her cold words, he had no trouble shoving it in her to
the roots, which made her gasp and say something that
sounded a lot sweeter in her own soft lingo. He didn't
need a translator to tell him what to do next. He just
hooked an elbow under each of her shapely knees,
spread her tawny naked thighs as wide as he could get
'em, and proceeded to pound her to glory as she kept
gasping, *"Wa, wa, wa!"*

He knew she wasn't crying, even if it sounded like

she might be. The Cheyenne had picked up "wa" from their Lakota allies. In either language, wa meant swell. By the time he had her coming, she'd flung both arms about him and was kissing him fit to bust. When she felt him ejaculate in her and keep going, she moaned in pleased surprise, and if she wasn't saying mighty nice things about him in Cheyenne it still *sounded* mighty sweet. But her voice seemed colder, if not as cold as before, when she switched back to English to demand, "Let me get on top, you big moose. The earth below my tailbone is hard, hard, and I do not want the other women laughing at me when I bathe in the morning. I know they will if you leave bruises on me down there!"

He said he sure wouldn't want anyone laughing at anything so pretty. He exchanged positions with her. The woolly robe under his own bare behind felt firm but not really hard enough to worry about bruises, until she got on top and really got to bouncing, as if she thought she was a pile driver and that he belonged ten feet underground. He'd feared, while on top, he might have been pounding her smaller body too roughly with his own. But now he saw why she'd really wanted to get on top. He could well believe she hadn't been getting much since her man went under at White River a few winters back. For her strong young body just couldn't seem to slam against his hard enough to satisfy her.

She ran out of breath once she'd climaxed that way. But he was still fixing to and so, knowing how tough she really was, now, he rolled her off, remounted her right, and just let himself go. As he did so she moaned, "Wa, now you are treating me like a real woman! Do you always hold back like that with your own kind?"

He came, let all his weight go limp atop her muscular

curves, and murmured, "Some gals don't get as much outdoor exercise as you. Are we pals, now?"

She hugged him tightly with her thighs and answered, "Don't be silly. This has nothing to do with warfare." Then she bit down teasingly with her internal muscles and added, in a softer musing tone, "You do this good, good, for an enemy, though."

So by the time they'd finished again they were talking to one another friendly enough for Longarm to risk her suggestion that they try for some shut-eye. If she cut his throat in his sleep he'd likely never know she had and, what the hell, if Little Wolf had outright murder in mind, they'd have never treated him to such a fine supper and grander dessert.

But it seemed to Longarm he'd barely dozed off before his gracious hostess was shaking him awake and whispering in his ear. He yawned, said he'd try, and reached for her in the inky darkness to roll her in for another round. That was when he noticed she'd put her deerskins back on. She cuddled closer, but told him softly, "I was able to get to your pony, unseen. It waits for you just outside, saddled and bridled. Someone else took the rifle you had tied to your saddle. But the bedroll is still there."

He yawned up at one star peeking down at them through the smoke ears and muttered, "It's pitch dark out, honey. How come you want to throw me out at this hour?"

"It's your only chance. They plan to feed you and even smoke with you after sunrise. Then, after you ride out in peace, a war band Little Wolf can say he knows nothing about is supposed to jump you, out on the open prairie. I think that if you leave now, and make it to the

27

timbered slopes of the Big Horn Mountains before day-break dawns on your pony tracks, you may have some chance. What do you think?"

He said, "I think I'd best get going. Where's my damned old boots?"

She started handing things to him in the dark as he got armed and dressed again. He didn't ask why she hadn't poked up the fire. The last thing he needed was light on the subject when he shoved aside the flap and slipped out. She followed as he did so. The sky read around four in the morning. The eastern skyline was already going oyster gray. By the little light it offered as she followed him to the pony she'd tethered to a nearby cottonwood, he saw her cheeks were wet. He hauled her in and kissed her, no matter what the local custom might be. He said, "I won't forget this, you sweet little enemy. Is this likely to make trouble for you with the others?"

She shook her head and said, "Just go. I can tell them you were gone when I woke up, later. But not if you don't get away. So what are you waiting for?"

He let go, untethered his Indian Agency bay, and led it afoot through the trees, away from the river, until he was out of easy earshot from light-sleeping Cheyenne who might not like him as much as Dancing Moon. Then he mounted up to ride for the safety of the wooded ridges to the west.

That is, he did so until he'd loped himself more wide awake. Then he reined in, drew his .44-40, and checked the cylinder by feel. Once he had he swore softly and reloaded the gun she'd emptied on him with fresh rounds from his coat pocket, muttering to his pony, "You're sure lucky to be a gelding, pard. There's just no end to the tricks womankind sees fit to play on us poor brutes with balls."

Then he reholstered his side arm and heeled his pony into a mile-eating if uncomfortable trot, due south instead of closer to the foothills to the west. He rode that way until he figured he was south of the strung-out camp along the Tongue. Then he cut east, toward the same river and, when they reached it, he got off again to lead his mount, afoot, along the sandy shallows of the Tongue. It was getting lighter by the minute, damn it, but it was still dark enough to lead his pony north, past the dark and brooding lodges of Little Wolf's camp. Somewhere in the night a dog commenced to bark. But it didn't seem to be barking at him. He murmured to the pony he was leading, "If you let out one fool sound at a time like this, you figure to spend the rest of your days as a wild Indian's pony, and you know we treat you better."

The pony, soothed by Longarm's tone if not his words, behaved just right until, farther downstream, Longarm remounted and rode on north, down the shallows, until sunrise caught them miles from the camp, surrounded by hopefully empty prairie, too summer-killed and sunbaked for easy tracking. He still made sure they left no obvious sign as they eased up out of the riverbed. Then he aimed them due east and beelined for the safety of the paleface settlements around Sheridan, feeling older but no wiser about current Indian problems.

The Indians were confused as well by this time. Back in camp Little Wolf was questioning Dancing Moon about her failure to set Longarm up for that ambush in the foothills. She was crying as she insisted, "Hear me. I did everything you told me to do. I even *lied* to him."

Little Wolf sighed and said, "Maybe it is just as well. He must have very strong medicine, like they say."

Dancing Moon looked away as she murmured to herself with a little smile, "He has other powers only Man'tou could have given him as well."

Chapter 3

The Burlington tracks ran half a day's ride east of Little Wolf's hidden camp, in line with the mountains though just distant enough from them to avoid cutting and grading for a more or less level right-of-way. The country still rolled enough for someone to have noticed outcrops of soft coal. So the railroad stop at Sheridan had grown into a fair-sized cattle- and coal-mining town by now.

As he rode in from the north along the tracks, Longarm knew he'd be stuck in Sheridan at least one afternoon, and that the Grand Paris Hotel had camping on open range beat by a mile even when the Indians were behaving themselves. But while the Grand Paris was the best hotel in town, he put off checking in there. They'd had a dining room waitress called Kitty working there the last time he'd stayed, not all that long ago and, while she screwed like a mink, a wise player seldom came back to the same table after he'd left it ahead of the game.

Kitty wasn't sore at him, he hoped. They'd parted friendly indeed after a night of friendly slap-and-tickle up in his hired room. But old Kitty would surely expect a rematch if she knew he was back in town, and she didn't get off until midnight. After all he'd been through without much sleep, of late, Longarm just didn't feel up to waiting up that late for a gal who, come to study on it, was no real beauty until you got her duds off.

He owed a courtesy call to the local law before he did anything less serious, in any event. So he left his jaded mount at a livery near the Western Union office and tipped the colored stable hand a whole two bits to make sure the bay was rubbed down as well as watered and oated. He let Western Union go for now. His boss, Marshal Billy Vail of the Denver District Court, just hated to pay for collect telegrams that didn't tell him a thing he didn't already now. Old Billy didn't know about old Dancing Moon, of course. But Western Union wouldn't let you send dirty wires and Longarm hadn't made up his mind about her band yet. They hadn't hurt him and he could have guessed wrong about her trying to set him up. He knew where they were if ever he wanted to tell the army about 'em. So they could simmer on the back of the stove for now.

He knew the town law of old and they were on good terms, since the local authorities had been understanding about a gunfight he'd once had on the platform of the nearby railroad stop. But when he got to the town lockup the peace officers he knew were out riding posse with the county sheriff. The young deputy left to hold down the desk with his spurred and booted feet shifted the match stem he was chewing to the other side of his mouth and told Longarm, "The sheriff's going to want to jaw with you, too, when he gets back. This being the county seat, he felt sort of left out the last time you passed through here, shooting. This being an election year, he'll no doubt want his picture took with such a famous visitor. How come they sent you all the way up from Denver *this* time, Deputy Long?"

Longarm sighed and said, "I wish Billy Vail

wouldn't do that. I got plenty of pals in Denver, male and female, but he will lend me out to other federal departments. This time I seem to be working for the B.I.A. again. Indian Affairs seems to admire the way I've somehow managed to keep their Indians and the War Department out of each other's hair a time or more."

The town deputy shifted his match stem again and said, "I figured that had to be it. The sheriff and our own old Dave will no doubt want to jaw with you on Indian matters as soon as they get back from riding in circles."

Longarm asked who the posse might be riding after and the kid replied, "Indians, of course. They hit a cattle spread just down the line near Cedar Creek near sunrise. Took some hair, this time."

Longarm whistled softly and asked, "How far south are we jawing about?" When the Sheridan lawman told him forty miles sounded about right, Longarm nodded and said, "I'd say that lets the only Cheyenne I know in these parts off. A sixty-mile ride ain't impossible. But I circled that Cheyenne camp on the Upper Tongue before I rode in, and since I did so by broad-ass daylight, I reckon I'd have noticed if a big war party had ridden out all that recent."

The younger lawman with his feet on the desk nodded and said, "We've been keeping an eye on Little Wolf. So far, and lucky for him, his band ain't been hunting east of the Tongue all summer. The wire for help we got this morning mentioned some arrows with green medicine stripes. Don't the Cheyenne stripe their arrows blue, like Blackfeet?"

Longarm nodded and said, "We're a mite south for Blackfoot, and while Arapaho admire green stripes more than Cheyenne might, the Arapaho seldom stray this side of the North Platte."

The local lawman pointed out, "That's talking peacetime, of course. I hear tell some Arapaho hit Custer, even farther north than we are now."

Longarm nodded but said, "Not that many and not that comfortable. The traditional hunting grounds of the Arapaho have ever been the big triangle of open grasslands formed by the North and South Platte. Aside from which they're a small nation and never really had their heart set on assassination. Both the army and most Indian agents agree the Arapaho chiefs seem more reasonable or at least more fatalistic than most. I wish I knew whether the Arapaho had a Contrary Lodge or not, though. Next to just about any Contrary, Red Cloud or Crazy Horse could qualify as a kindly old philosopher."

The kid asked if Contraries were the Indians who rode at you left-handed and backwards. Longarm didn't want to get into such a tedious lecture on a subject he didn't really know, so he said that was close enough, added that he hadn't had breakfast, and that he'd drop by later, once the posse got back.

They both knew that didn't figure to be soon. After riding a good forty miles and then in any number of circles, seeking sign, the long-gone posse figured to camp down around Cedar Creek overnight. Nobody with a lick of sense would want to try a long night ride with Indians lurking all about in the dark. Nobody but the dudes back-east who wrote army manuals bought that shit about the Indians never attacking after dark. Big war parties didn't like to charge on horseback after dark any more than the U.S. Cav did. But the night was made for sneak attacks and the Contraries were said to do most anything, at any time, in any event.

Longarm found a beanery that served beer as well as chili con carne and apple pie. Feeling hungrier than usual he asked the Greek short-order cook to slip a slab of ham under the chili and maybe a couple of fried eggs on top. The Greek said it was his stomach, as long as he had six bits, and stared at him in both awe and dismay as Longarm demolished the unusual repast. Longarm could see the fool foreigner hadn't been out west all that long. But he'd never met a Greek or Chinaman who couldn't cook pretty good. So he didn't tease the poor pilgrim. He just topped off his second slice of pie with three cups of black coffee and left the beanery feeling better than its owner seemed to.

The day was still young, but not young enough for him to think of anything sensible to do to kill the time until the posse got back. He resisted the temptation to hire a fresh mount at the livery and tear south to join the sheriff and his riders. He knew he'd have a time catching up with them whether he could make Cedar Creek by sundown or not. But fighting the restless urge served to remind him that some other boyfriend of Dancing Moon no doubt now had the rifle he'd started out with. So when he spied the sign of a gunsmith just down the way he headed for it, rehearsing the way he meant to bargain for a used Winchester, or at least a Henry if they'd throw in a box of free .44-40.

But when he entered the narrow and cluttered shop, and a bell above the door summoned the management from the back rooms, he saw that once again he'd wasted practice on a conversation that might not go at all the way he'd rehearsed it. He had to cross out a lot of the dirty words he was primed to use when beating down the price of a pony or a used gun. For the sweet-smiling little thing with her auburn hair bunned atop her

fine-boned head looked like she'd blush or even cry if a
man asked her how much she wanted for that rusty old
length of pure shit they were advertising as a Winchester in the window.

Knowing and suspecting she knew it was plain unfair
to make a man bargain with a pretty woman, Longarm
smiled back at her and said, "Howdy. Some Cheyenne
stole my saddle gun. So I'm in the market for a new
one, by which I mean a used one in fair shape. How
much are you asking for that Winchester out front?"

The little gunsmith, or maybe his daughter, talked
soprano as most gals, but put things more like a down-
home gun monger as she replied, "You don't want that
one if I'm reading the frayed lapel of your frock coat
right. That silver inlay is for a top hand who can afford
silver-mounted spurs as well. Am I correct in assuming
you'd be a lawman in need of a shooting iron instead of
a thing of beauty?"

Longarm laughed and said, "I'm sure glad I ain't a
flirtatious husband married to you, no offense. For one
blonde or brunette hair on this beat-up tweed would
likely cook my goose."

He hauled out his wallet, opened it to show her his
I.D. and the badge he kept pinned inside it when he
wasn't trying to impress redskins, and added, "This is
what you missed when you told me so polite I could use
new duds as well as a fresh saddle gun, ma'am. I'll
want a receipt written out in my official name, when
and if we strike a bargain. My office won't pay me back
for the unforeseen expense unless you put everything
down plain."

She blinked in surprise and said, "Good heavens, are
you the famous marshal they call Longarm?"

He winced and said, "I'm only a deputy marshal. My

boss, the one and original U.S. Marshal Billy Vail, gets to sit at a desk all day while us old boys do all the work and lose all the guns. But I have to plead guilty to being called Longarm by some. Does that make me famous, in your book?"

She dimpled and told him, "In *this* business? It certainly does! Colt and Winchester both brag on you a lot, and as soon as I sell you a gun from this very shop *I* mean to brag on it with a sign in the window. My handle would be Norma Fraser, by the by."

They shook on that and then she turned about to mount a stepladder, calling back to him, "I've got just the saddle gun for a boy your size and I can let you have her at cost, seeing as you'd be such a distinguished customer."

He admired the view she made coming down even better. For she had to sway more in her thin black poplin skirts with both hands full of considerable gun. As she turned to place it on the glass counter between them Longarm cocked an eyebrow and said, "It sure looks *long,* ma'am. To tell the truth, I had something like a Henry or Winchester in mind."

She shook her head firmly and insisted, "Not if you mean to mess with Indians on the Wyoming range. Most of this *is* a Winchester, ordered special for a customer who never came back to pick it up. The action's the same. It takes the same shells, albeit more of 'em in its longer magazine. The extra inches of barrel add up to twenty-one shots flying true as a target rifle."

Longarm picked up the clumsy looking saddle gun and hefted it dubiously. Then he grinned and said, "I'll be switched with snakes if I don't like the balance of this freak Winchester. How come it ain't as muzzle-heavy as it ought to be, ma'am?"

She said modestly, "I took off the butt plate, drilled me a few holes in the stock, and filled 'em with molten lead until I made up for the extra length the factory added. I zeroed in the sights for the longer range while I was at it. She'll carry a good three hundred yards with no guesswork on your part. Would you like to test it, out back, before we talk price?"

He said that sounded fair, and as she proceeded to load it full for him he asked, "How much gunsmithing do they allow you to do here, ma'am?"

She shrugged and said, "All of it. There's no they I have to answer to. I own this place, lock, stock and barrel." Then she handed the rifle-length carbine to him, its muzzle of course aimed at the ceiling with no round in the chamber and the safety lock on. He kept things that way as she reached under her counter and came around to join him with a .22 Remington revolver in her left hand, saying, "I just can't stand to watch a customer have all the fun. Follow me and I'll pick us up some cans from my kitchen to shoot at."

But that wasn't the way things went. For just then they both heard a fusillade of gunfire out front, and the pretty gunsmith gasped, "Oh, Lord, I fear they're holding up the bank again!"

Longarm didn't answer. He just stepped out the front of her shop, levering a round into the chamber of the gun she was trying to sell him and snapping off the safety as, sure enough, a half-dozen riders with feed sacks over their faces came down the dusty street at full gallop, throwing lead and war whoops in every damn careless direction. So Longarm just did what any sensible lawman should have at such times, and he was more than surprised when the two last riders rolled out of their saddles before he could get around to either with his swell new saddle gun.

His ears still ringing from the roar of the four serious rounds he'd thrown—as well as that fool .22 going off almost in his ear—Longarm told the lady with the pistol, "I'll take this Winchester if you'll promise never to throw spitballs at armed and dangerous criminals no more. I'd best go have a look-see at what we just wrought."

He wasn't too surprised when little Norma tagged along at his left side while he strode out to the center of the street as the dust was still settling and a crowd was commencing to gather from all sides. The outlaws' ponies had run off for now. The four he'd shot were about in the shape one expected a gent to be in after he'd taken a bruising round of .44-40 in the chest and fallen off a horse. The two Norma had nailed looked neat next to their pals until Longarm hauled their feed sacks off and said flatly, "That was damned fine shooting, ma'am."

He meant it. Luck could have explained one pair of dead eyes staring cross-eyed at the bullet hole between 'em. But to drill two men aboard running ponies the exact same way, a man, or in this case a woman, had to know exactly what he or she was doing.

Norma said soberly, "I hope I did the right thing. I saw you were shooting at them and— Oh, dear, what if they wasn't out to rob the bank after all?"

Longarm told her soothingly, "I doubt they were riding into town for more innocent fun. I know these two of old as federal wants. Let's see how many of the Clifford Gang we got in all."

As he was shucking the masks of the other dead owlhoots, the young deputy they'd left to mind the store showed up just in time to tell a couple of muttering townsmen that it was all right for Longarm to be doing that. Then he told Longarm, "It's sure a good thing you was down this way to cut 'em off, Longarm. The rascals knew our lockup was on the far side of the bank. One of 'em ought to have another feed sack full of money."

Longarm said, "It's likely tied to the horn of a pony that ought to be slowing down any time now." The town deputy just stood there looking green as he likely was. But a couple of townee boys yelled like dog soldiers and started running down the street to recover the dead men's mounts.

The town law started to run after them. Then he stopped and turned back to Longarm and Norma, saying, "This is the first time I've been in charge during a shoot-out. What am I supposed to do next, Longarm?"

It was tempting. Longarm just hated paperwork. But the kid had yet to do him dirt. So he felt he owed it to a fellow lawman to enlighten him. He grimaced and said, "First you have these dead gents hauled over to the county coroner. That's how we done it the last time I had to gun a gunslick in your fair city. The old doc I recall from the last time knows his job. He'll know how to write things up for his records. If the local boy who catches up with the right pony is halfway honest he'll return the money direct to the bank or to you. He's supposed to turn it over to you. But you'd only have to tote it to the bank yourself, so don't fuss at him if he saves you the trip."

Then he took Norma by her free right arm and announced, "In the meantime I got to settle up with Lefty, here, for this good old Winchester I hadn't got about to buying, yet. You all go on about your business and I'll join you at the coroner's in just a few minutes. I know the way from last time."

Nobody argued. So he got the gunsmith alone in her gun shop and shut the door after them before he said, "There's more than one way to skin this cat, little pard, and I was brung up to allow ladies to choose what might happen next."

"Anyone can see you're a gent of the old school. But would you mind telling me what we're talking about?"

"Bounty money," he said. "I didn't want to make your skill with a .22 a matter of record without your permit. But if you don't mind taking the credit, and the money as goes with six dead-or-alive fliers, we can make you rich and save me an infernal county inquest if we go to face the music together, see?"

She must not have. She said, "I'm not worried about my rep in these parts. I'd rather have 'em whisper about me killing a few men than doing what they always say a good-looking young widow woman does to men with wives of their own. How much do you reckon I'll get for the two I shot, Custis?"

Longarm said, "Six. You shot all six of the Clifford boys, and there was roughly six or eight hundred posted on each of 'em." He counted rapidly in his head before he added, "Let's call her four thousand as a round numbers minimum. Could you use it?"

She looked a heap happier than she'd ever looked since he'd laid eyes on her as she replied, "Oh, Lord, could I ever! Trade has been just dreadful since my man was taken from me more than a year ago. Some customers just can't get it through their thick skulls that a woman knows a thing about guns and— Hold on, what might *you* get out of laying all of the gang on my doorstep, you mighty friendly old pussycat?"

41

Longarm said, "I don't lose nothing. My department frowns on us federal deputies putting in for bounty money and, hey, don't you reckon we ought to keep all the money in the family?"

She asked him to wait while she put on her bonnet. But as they were leaving for the coroner's office behind the courthouse she sighed and said, "It's not going to work. There's just no way a round of .44-40 is going to pass for a .22 Long when they cut those boys open on the autopsy tables."

"Not if anyone looks that hard. It's worth a try. I found old Doc Wortham an understanding cuss the last time I passed through Sheridan. I suspect he likes his paperwork as short and simple as I do."

By this time they were out in the sunlight and headed the right way. But Norma didn't seem in any hurry to get there as she said, "You don't get to deal with Doc Wortham, this time. He's been laid up a good month or more with an unmentionable social disease."

Longarm raised an eyebrow to ask, "Do tell? He struck me as a decent old gent to be coming down with the . . . unmentionables."

Norma sighed and said, "He is. He caught it doing an autopsy on a fancy gal as died from the same. His assistant, the snip we'll have to deal with, is that snooty Miss Mira Hecht, a not exactly ugly but mighty bossy German gal!"

Longarm thought back, nodded, and said, "I recall her if she's a sort of frosty ash-blonde. She never gave me no trouble. On the other hand she wasn't in charge. You say you and her are enemies, you straight-shooting little thing?"

Norma shook her head as she answered, "That would be putting it a mite strong. We only know one another to

42

nod in passing. But I've heard a lot about her and her German temper, so—"

"So she's no doubt heard about your merry-widow ways with all the men in town," Longarm cut in. "She didn't act all that bossy with me, when last we met, and whether her name is German or Chinese she talked plain American enough for me to savvy. I suspect she had to go to high school, at least, to get a job as assistant county coroner. Sometimes folk without much book learning take proper English as snooty manners, or at least an excuse for a fight. Let me do the talking and we can likely get her to see things our way."

They moved on. It was a good thing Norma had been such a reluctant walker. For they were carrying the last cadaver in from the buckboard as the couple who'd left them in that condition arrived. Mira Hecht was standing in the side doorway, looking stiff and starched in her linen autopsy smock with a rubber apron down the front. She had her long blonde hair bunned up out of the way, too. She nodded at Norma and grimaced at Longarm as she asked, "Don't you ever pass through Sheridan without shooting anyone, Deputy Long? It was bad enough last time, but this time you've really overdone it."

Longarm ticked the brim of his hat to her and replied, "Look on the bright side, Miss Mira. What would you do for a living in such a healthy climate if nobody never got shot? But don't fuss at me, this time, ma'am. It was Miss Lefty, here, who done the good deed and rates all the rewards of her honest effort."

Mira looked startled and said, "That's not what they just told me about the gunfight in front of the gun shop, Deputy Long."

He shrugged and said, "Call me Custis, since I surely hope we're all on the same side here. Nobody but Miss

43

Norma and me was close enough to see just what was going on. I'll have to confess I pegged a few shots, albeit with a new gun she was showing me. Balance must have been off. My little pard emptied all six saddles with her target pistol, see?"

The cool blonde said, "We'll see, inside. Where might either of the guns you mentioned be right now? All I see is that wicked .44-40 you're still wearing under that same shabby coat."

As she led them inside, Longarm explained they'd left both the rifle-length carbine and .22 pistol at the gun shop. Mira said, "No matter. I can always ask to see them later, should there be any problem with the probable causes of death I have to sign."

By this time the men who'd brought the bodies to the morgue had stripped all six, placed two atop the zinc tables under the skylight, and seemed to be trying not to grin as they waited for further orders. Mira glanced down at the amazingly well hung as well as naked body on the far table, grimaced, and said, "My, he was quite a man, wasn't he?" She casually plunged her shiny steel scalpel into him, deep, just above the pubic bone and proceeded to rip him open to the breastbone, adding, "Hand me that saw hanging behind you, will you, Nick?"

The tough-looking Nick looked away as he placed the bone saw in her rubber-gloved hand and headed for the door for some fresher air if not a place to puke. The others commenced to drift out as she sawed the cadaver's ribs open to each nipple and, having made the standard grim Y incision, proceeded to gut the dead outlaw as if she planned on serving him for the coming Thanksgiving. Norma had to turn away with a shudder. Mira asked her sweetly, "What's the matter, dear? Did you think those guns you sell only cause a slight rash?"

Then she hauled out a bone-flattened .44-40 slug, held it up to the light, and asked Longarm, "Is this your idea of a .22 target round?"

Longarm sighed and said, "It's for you to say, Miss Mira. I ain't allowed to put in for bounty money and *somebody* ought to get it, don't you agree?"

The tall willowy blonde did stare sort of like a German drillmaster, come to study on it, as she stuck her blade in the other corpse for safekeeping. Then she turned and strode over to a wall cabinet cluttered with bitty boxes, cups, and tin cans. She dropped Longarm's slug in a can with an ominous clatter, rummaged about for yet another can, and moved back to the table. She held the can out to Longarm, saying, "I want you to hold this and act as witness, should it ever come up." Then she dropped a bitty .22 slug in the can he could have sworn rattled more when she'd first picked it up. Norma didn't catch on at first, since she knew she'd fired a .22 round at two of them. She chose not to watch as Mira took a second ".22" from the second one Longarm had downed and got him to help her exchange the body for a fresh one from the floor. When she sliced its torso open and dropped the third .22 in the can, Norma turned with a bemused look, gagged at the sliced-open horror between them, but worked up the grit to keep staring, wide eyed, as the frosty assistant coroner somehow found the fourth chest-shot man had been hit by a .22.

It was hard for even Longarm to watch as the expressionless, cool blonde recovered the last two real slugs from Norma's bitty pistol from the last two skulls, with her saw doing most of the work. When she'd dropped exactly six .22 slugs in the can, she said, "That ought to satisfy the county. I can't see any heirs coming forward to dispute my findings, can you?"

Longarm smiled thinly and said, "Not hardly, Miss Mira. Anyone can see you're mighty skilled at forensic science. Your sleight of hand ain't bad, neither."

She shot him a drillmaster look indeed and told him flatly, "I don't know what you're talking about. My report will simply read that all six bank robbers were shot in a lawful manner by one or more responsible citizens, and add that since both the Widow Fraser and a federal lawman agree she nailed four in the upper thorax and two in the crania, this office sees no reason to dispute her and her witness. You do see the bullets I removed from all the bodies appear to be identical, don't you, witness?"

Longarm managed to keep a straight face—it wasn't easy—as he nodded soberly and said, "That oughta hold 'em. What do you want me to sign, Miss Mira?"

The blonde shrugged and said, "Later, after I get it all typed up. All the undertaker needs for some fast and shallow shovel work in Potter's Field are the standard death certificates. I can file the rest any old time." Then she shot him an amused look and said, "You'd better make that around suppertime, at my place up Flint Street near Collier. Knowing you, I'd like to feel sure you'll be around to sign anything. You'd best come, too, Miss Norma. I'll need both your John Hancocks. Any questions?"

Norma gulped and asked, "I have one. How come you ain't been as cold to me as I was led to expect?"

The taller gal shrugged and said, "I only treat folk sort of ugly when they wind up on one of my tables. You've never done anything to spite me. Why would I have call to spite you?"

46

Then she stripped off her gloves, reached under her apron for a clean kerchief and handed it to Norma, saying, "Here. Never cry in front of menfolk. The brutes already think they're tougher than us."

Norma covered her face with the white linen and ran outside, bawling fit to bust. Longarm told Mira, "That was mighty decent of you, ma'am. I didn't want to say it in front of her, but she's been having a hard time at her gun shop since her brute died."

Mira sighed and said, "Did you really think I perjured myself as a favor to *you*? You brutes can take care of yourselves. But some small-town gossip is true. The bank she just saved all that money for was fixing to foreclose on her mortgage. Do you think the miserly money on these miserable thieves will tide her over until business picks up?"

Longarm said, "Yep. Next to buying a gun from a big tough brute there's nothing as reassuring as buying said gun off a woman that shoots mighty fine with her own stock. I'd best get her on back now, lest she rust my new saddle gun with all that blubbering."

She didn't act as if she minded. He moved over to the door. Then he turned, removed his Stetson entire, and said, "I'd have to blubber some too, if us brutes was allowed to. Would it upset you if I told you I thought you was a good old gal, Miss Mira?"

She told him not to talk mush. He said, "The simple truth ain't mush, Miss Mira. You ought to smile more often and let the world see what a nice lady you are." Then he left before she could throw a basin of blood or worse at him.

Norma hadn't run off far. He found her red-eyed just outside and said, "That wasn't so bad, was it? I'll just carry you back to your shop, settle up about that saddle gun, and get out of the way before the stampede commences. By this time tomorrow there won't be a man in this county with a busted gun that won't want it fixed by the gunsmith who wiped out the Clifford Gang, left-handed."

As they walked back arm-in-arm she sniffed and said, "It's only beginning to hit me. I didn't know what a load I had on my shoulders until you and that sweet Mira Hecht lifted it off me just now. But Custis, I feel so mean and ashamed."

He said he didn't see why. So she said, "I have *spited* Mira, more than once. I fear I've been just as mean mouthed about her as the other ladies in town. At least, I never *argued* when other ladies called her a stuck-up square-head."

He chuckled and said, "I'd hardly say such mean-mouthing gals were *ladies*. Gossips with nothing better to do is all I can come up with. If prim manners were all they could come up with to use in her disfavor, I'd say *she* was the lady and hadn't been spited more than usual. I hope it's shown you not to judge a book by its cover. I've learned not to do that. You see, they invited me to a war one time, before I'd finished school. So, to make up for it, I read a lot when nobody's looking."

She shot a look up at him and decided, "You can't mean you rode in the Civil War, Custis. You don't look that old!"

"I ain't. I was way too young when I ran off to the war. I might not have acted so dumb if I'd been any older. If it was up to me they wouldn't take nobody under thirty or forty into any fool army. For one thing, it would sure cut down on wars that men too old to fight in love to declare." Then he spied the stuffy gent in a snuff frock coat and stovepipe hat waiting for them by the locked door of her gun shop and muttered, "Speaking of broody looking old men. . . ."

She said, "Oh, dear, that's banker Hawkins and he surely does have a mean look in his eye, doesn't he?"

Longarm replied softly that it was hard to tell, once a man had been born so ugly. Then they were too close to comment on the tight-lipped old fart. Hawkins at least had the grace to tip his hat to Norma and then slap it back on lest they notice his bald head. Norma said, "How nice to see you, sir. I hope it's not on business, this early in the month."

The sour-faced Hawkins said, "I fear it is, my dear. The matter of the mortgage you and your late husband took out with us came up at the board meeting we just had this afternoon, and I was delegated to approach you about it."

Norma almost sobbed, "Can't you wait just a few more days, sir? As you may have heard, I'm expecting some reward money any time now. But I fear I can't even pay my coal bill at this time of the month."

Before Longarm could even look scary at him, the stuffy old cuss said, "Oh, heavens, did you think I'd come here to *ask* you for money, dear child?"

Norma seemed too confused to answer. So Longarm did, steely voiced, "What *are* you doing here, then?"

To which the banker replied, "To *thank* the little lady, of course! The money those outlaws took from Drover's Trust has just been recovered, and even if it hadn't been, this brave young woman made sure the Clifford Gang will never rob us or anyone else again!"

Before Norma could put her foot in her mouth, Longarm said, "I noticed. Saying thank you won't even get you a smile from the waitress in a decent beanery, unless you leave something more solid for her."

He was braced for an argument. The banker spoiled all his fun by nodding and saying, "We at the bank agree." Then he turned back to Norma and asked, "Would you consider it fair if we just canceled your mortgage, Miss Norma? It does come to a tidy sum, you know, what with all the extensions, at interest, we've had to extend since your late husband's demise."

She said, "I know full well, sir. I mean to pay it off in time but I have to have *more* time!"

The banker and Longarm exchanged glances. Longarm said, "I reckon she's still excited about the shoot-out. We just came from the coroner's. Are you saying she's off the hook, pure and simple, with no outstanding debts at all?"

Hawkins nodded and said, "Of course. We agreed it seemed highly unlikely she'd ever pay off such an ill-advised mortgage, and we agreed at the same time we'd hardly be Christian if we foreclosed on a struggling young widow who foiled the robbery of our very bank. So—"

"She wants a quitclaim, in writing," Longarm cut in, smiling polite. "No offense, Christian. But as a lawman I've seen how sudden a local hero can be forgotten, and you do have her down on paper as owing you considerable with this bitty shop as the security, right?"

Hawkins flushed and said, "I can't say I admire your manners, young sir. Did you really think you had to tell a banker how such transactions should be carried out?"

Then, before Longarm could reply that somebody ought to, the mean-faced old man whipped a neatly folded sheaf of bond paper from under his coat and presented it to Norma with another tip of his stovepipe, saying, "This is your quitclaim, dear, signed and notarized. You'll find your little shop is now all yours, free and clear, unless your lawyer, here, wants to argue some more about it."

As Norma clutched the papers to her bosom with a glad little cry, Longarm held out his hand to Hawkins, saying, "My apologies, sir, and I mean it. I fear I was just guilty of a sin I'd just warned someone else about. It's just plain dumb to judge a book by its cover and that's what I just done."

Hawkins shook with him, firmly, and managed a lopsided grin as he replied, "I know what I look like, and to tell the truth, I don't think *you're* all that pretty either."

So they all laughed like hell and parted friendly.

Inside, as Longarm reloaded the special Winchester he'd left on the counter, Norma beamed up at him through tear-filled eyes and told him *she* thought he was pretty as hell, explaining, "You can't fool me with that country act of yours, Custis. You may look cow and talk cow, but under all that hayseed you're so smart it's sort of scary. It seems less than an hour ago you came in here to buy a gun, and now here I stand with my mortgage paid off, even more cash coming, and I suspect you're right about my business picking up a lot. Don't you *ever* mess up?"

He said he sure did. But he was too polite to explain how a man might mess up with a sweet little widow woman smiling up at him so tender. He knew himself at least as well as he could read the smoke signals in her big green teary eyes. So before he could get them both in trouble he said, "I got to get on up the road, ma'am. How much do I owe you for this freak Winchester?"

She said, "Heavens! Don't be silly! If, thanks to you, the bank can give me back my mortgage, I 'spect I have the right to give away guns to my friends. I only wish there was some other way I could repay you, you darling man!"

He said the gun would be more than he deserved and reached behind him for the door latch. He'd no more than grabbed it when little Norma stood on tiptoe to kiss him flush on the mouth. It happened too fast for him to respond in full, praise the Lord. So when she dropped back on her heels, blushing, to say, "There! I just had to do that!" he was able to tell her she sure kissed swell and got out of there before she could kiss him again, or vice versa. He was already feeling wistful about his common sense by the time he'd taken ten steps.

But then, on the eleventh, a young cowhand on a lathered roan came tearing down the street, yelling, "Massacre! Indian massacre out to the Rocking Seven!" and Longarm was able to put other temptations aside for now.

Chapter 4

Longarm ran catty-corner to the livery, shoved the special Winchester into the saddle boot the lost one belonged in, and got the stable hands to put it, saddle and all, aboard a fresh mount. As he mounted up and headed for the lockup, where he figured they'd be most likely to posse-up, he made a mental note to tip those horse-wise colored gents better, when and if he got back to his Indian Agency pony again. For they'd picked him a mighty fine remount.

It was a chunky cordovan gelding with Morgan lines. It responded willingly to the gentle hand he preferred to use on the reins. It led with its off forehoof, as a well-trained cow or cavalry pony was supposed to, and had a predictable and hence comfortable lope. Longarm could feel the muscular hind quarters had a lot of reserve steam in them. The stable hands had told him the critter was as fast as it needed to be at any given time. But since this time they only had to lope a short ways, they'd barely met one another before Longarm reined in near the cluster of pony rumps in front of the lockup.

He dismounted, tethered the cordovan to a lamppost, and went on in where, sure enough, the young town deputy was holding court to a dozen-odd assorted coal and cattle workers. As he saw Longarm coming in he rose from behind his desk and said, "Praise the Lord you showed up, Longarm. With both the town and county law out of town to the south, we got to posse north, and to tell the truth, I've never led a posse afore."

Longarm joined the small mob gathered about the desk and got a cheroot going before he said, "I hate to be the one as has to tell you. But you won't be leading one this afternoon if you have a lick of sense and any regard at all for the bank just up the way. I suspect that when they left you in charge here, it was with the distinct impression you'd keep an eye on the lives and property of Sheridan. A town this size has to have at least *one* peace officer on duty at all times, you know."

The kid stuck with the chore nodded but said, "We still have to do something about the massacre up the line to the north, damn it. What say you take these old boys out after them wild Indians?"

Longarm took a thoughtful drag on his smoke before he replied, "What say we study on the situation just a mite, first? If we're talking about a real uprising, nobody but a total asshole would go charging out this close to dusk when there's a Western Union just down the street and an army that just loves to chase Indians in considerable numbers. How many Indians are we talking about in the first place?"

A young cowhand wearing two six-guns over his North Plains goatskin chaps announced, "Nobody can say, for sure. The wrangler out to the Rocking Seven was the only one who got a good look at the red rascals, and he's dead. But he took one of 'em with him.

"The way me and the bunkhouse gang puts it together, old Bill caught 'em messing with our remuda when he went out back to check the watering troughs. They put a couple of arrows in old Bill to lay him low,

54

discreet. But the sign reads he hung on to a corral pole long enough to get his gun out and cripple-up one of the red bastards, at least. His shot drawed the rest of us outta the dinner shack afore we could finish our grub. We could see at a glance that old Bill was down and that a painted Indian was flopping about in the corral like a circus seal. So we finished him off, of course. Then we circled for sign and saw that while old Bill had saved our stock, a whole mess of ponies had just lit out for parts unknowed. That's when me and Will Waters bee-lined into town for help."

Longarm glanced at the wall clock to his left as he said, "I think I just met Will Waters, yelling something about a massacre. Saying you Rocking Seven hands set down for grub the usual time, around five, it took you less'n an hour to massacre that one red horse thief and get here. So we're talking a short distance out of town. But it'll still be pushing sundown by the time anyone can get back out to scout more sign. Are there any handy ambush sites like a deep wash or a railroad trestle between here and the Rocking Seven?"

The hand looked blank and replied, "Hell, no, it's a flat, open run between our spread and town. That's how come me and Will risked riding in alone for help."

Another man dressed cow said, "I follow Longarm's drift. Indian tactics do include drawing us poor boys into such grim scenes by hitting one place and laying low another."

Longarm calmed the resultant worried murmur with a wave of his cheroot and announced, "All right. That ain't what they had in mind. They were likely just after horseflesh and, if they left a wounded brother brave behind as they ran from the contents of one dinner shack, we can assume they were either a mighty small party or yellow as buttercups. I'm sorry about your poor wrangler. But I doubt they'll even try to lift any hair this close to this here county seat unless *all* the fighting men in town dash off to ride in circles in the dark."

The temporary town law nodded but protested, "Ain't we supposed to do *nothing* about a white man massacred by Indians, damn it?"

Longarm soothed, "Sure we are. As the senior peace officer in these parts at the moment, and seeing the killings took place on or close enough to federal open range, I'll ride out and see what I can scout this side of total darkness. If it reads like real Indian trouble I'll report it to the War Department. If it reads like a boyish prank I'll report it to the B.I.A. and let the Indian Police worry about it."

The junior deputy protested, "Hold on. It reads to me as if the very band of renegade raiders our sheriff and my boss chased after could be the ones as just hit the Rocking Seven!"

Longarm blew smoke out his nostrils in disgust and replied, "That's no doubt because you're still behind that desk instead of out on the range. Your sheriff and the others rode due south a good forty-odd miles, responding to an emergency they had no damn business responding to. But that's neither here nor there. The one and only way a war party could circle from Cedar Creek to north of Sheridan, in the time they had to work with, would be by riding fast and straight and to hell with any trail or dust they were leaving aboard mighty tired ponies. By afternoon light the sheriff and his posse would have spotted at least their dust from miles away. So where could all those Sheridan riders be at the moment if we're talking about the same Indians?"

Most of them seemed to follow his drift. A coal

miner didn't. So Longarm explained, "Assuming the same band, raiding a nearby cattle spread no more than an hour ago with a posse hot on their tails, don't you reckon the sheriff and his boys would have come home for supper by now?"

The coal miner nodded sheepishly and said, "Right. Unless we have winged Indian ponies to worry about, it has to be at least *two* war bands. That's easier to buy than winged ponies."

Longarm shrugged and said, "War bands may be putting it a mite strong. So far, nobody's spotted more than a dozen anything in a bunch. But there ain't much daylight left to work with. So I'd best ride out to the Rocking Seven and, Lord willing and they didn't split up, see if I can get a rough count and general direction, at least."

As he headed for the door with one of the hands who'd carried the news to town, some others volunteered to come along. But Longarm said, "You'd best stay here to hold the fort until that posse gets back. I'd say it was over out at the Rocking Seven. If it ain't, me and the boys they already run from ought to be able to hold thrice as many off, forted up inside."

Nobody argued. Longarm suspected more than one was secretly glad to be let off the hook. Men were always willing to scare the shit out of themselves lest someone call them sissies. The one called Will met them outside and the three of 'em mounted up.

The ride out to the cattle spread was short and across as open prairie as Wyoming had to offer. But it gave Longarm and his remount time to get to know each other better, and Longarm decided the cordovan was damned fine stock for a livery horse, even before young Bob, the one who wasn't Will, observed it surely seemed a frisky steed, considering how big Longarm was.

The sun hung low above the purple Big Horns to the west by the time they reined in near the corral of the Rocking Seven. But the light was still good, and although all the excitement was now close to two hours in the past, a couple of dozen excited riders were still milling about on foot, just in case they hadn't yet stomped and scattered any sign left to read. Young Bob called out that Longarm was the law, federal, and they all simmered down to gather round and treat him respectful.

He dismounted and tethered his mount to a corral rail upwind of the body he saw sprawled near the corral gate, with a six-gun in its hand and two arrows rising from the back of its checkered shirt. Longarm hunkered down to bust both arrows off for examination. The only way one could draw a barbed arrow out the way it had gone in was needlessly messy. One arrow had long faded medicine stripes that could have started out Cheyenne blue. The other shaft was newer and had never been painted. Longarm muttered to himself and anyone who wanted to listen, "Hunting arrows. They'd be fresh painted if the owner or owners had worked their fool selves up with drumming and dancing first. I'd say this old boy was hit from behind as he was throwing down on someone else out front. He never fired *after* he was arrowed. He was hit in the spine and the back door of his heart by a mighty good bowman."

Then he rose back to his full height, nodded at what looked sort of like a couple of yards of ground beef out in the corral, and said, "Let's see what the other body has to tell me, if that could be a body."

He rolled through the rails and, as he moved closer, he could see the dead whatever was chewed up worse than he'd thought from any distance in the orange light of gloaming. The mangled cadaver lay on its back, naked save a breechclout. He turned to young Bob and said, "I thought you told us your wrangler put no more than half a dozen rounds in this cuss and left him in a winged condition."

Another, harder looking hand said, "Old Bill only hit the son of a bitch once, in the hipbone. We finished him off entire, as you see. Looking back, I'd say we reloaded a time or two as we stood over him in a circle, pissing lead into him for what he done to our pard."

Longarm swallowed the green taste in his mouth, rinsed it out with some more smoke, and said softly, "I sure wish you'd left more of him for me to work with. Anyone can see his hide looks darker than our own, where it ain't been perforated. But I just can't say what his skull might have looked like before you boys smashed it like a pumpkin under a spiked steamroller."

Another hand said, "Oh, he looked Indian enough. I got a good look at his face, screaming, afore I emptied my gun into it."

The hard case who seemed to be their ramrod asked, "What the hell difference does it make, Longarm? Are you saying our poor wrangler might have caught a horse thief disguised as an Indian?"

Longarm shrugged and said, "It happens. Those arrows seem a mite artistic for a Mountain Meadows job, though. You say you had some pony tracks to show me?"

The ramrod nodded but said, "Just where the ground is bare, yonder way to the north. I told the boys not to walk on 'em."

Longarm nodded in approval and led the parade on foot to the far side of the corral. They all rolled through

59

the rails and, sure enough, anyone could see where at least six or eight ponies had milled some and then headed for the north pole or at least the unreadable dry stubble about fifty yards out. Longarm stopped at the edge of the grass and turned to peer back at the pony sign, etched clearly now by the slanting orange sunlight and purple shading. He mused aloud, "This just don't read sensible at all. Horse thieves of any description might know suppertime was as good a time as any to lift horseflesh. Had your wrangler been less attentive they'd have likely led a few head of stock right out the gate. After that it gets murky. Neither Indians nor experienced white stock stealers would have come this close aboard their own ponies. The way it's done is to hide your mounts out of sight and move in afoot. Worse yet, anyone can see they were riding shod ponies, and an assimilated Indian with a blacksmith in the family seldom bothers to shoe his mount for open grass country."

One of the hands asked, "What about Little Wolf's band, over on the far side of the Tongue? They hunt deer and elk in the more rocky Big Horns, don't they?"

Longarm frowned thoughtfully and said, "I was just over yonder and so I got a fair look-see at Little Wolf's camp. I didn't see one shod pony. That band is living sort of old-time religion, even for Cheyenne. The boys who hit here might have picked up some well-shod ponies in their travels. The ones they were trying to steal here all wear horseshoes. But it does make one wonder. I'm having a time picturing Indians of any nation who ride like greenhorn stock thieves and shoot arrows better than many an old Crooked Lance."

He was sorry he'd said that as they all mosied back the way they'd just come. The cattle industry had moved north to the Wyoming range as the buffalo and buffalo-hunting nations got shot off. He found it boring to lecture cowhands on Indian matters any white man within miles of any Indians left ought to know about already. He settled for saying, "Indians divvy up their military the same as we do our artillery, infantry, cav and so on. Only they do it more ceremonial. The Dog Soldier Lodge is sort of Indian M.P.s. The Crooked Lances are their shock troops."

The ramrod said, "That makes sense. Which, ah, lodge did poor old Custer mix with just north of here that time?"

Longarm said, "All kinds from all lodges. Never ride smack into a big Indian encampment unless you're ready to take on Dog Soldiers shooting at you from cover, Suicide Boys charging you on foot, and the riding lodges charging you from both flanks at the same time."

Before anyone could ask him to explain the Suicide Boys, or untested youths who weren't allowed to join any fighting lodge until they'd lifted hair or horseflesh on their own, someone else called out, "Buckboard coming in. From town, most likely."

Longarm peered over the hats of the hands between him and the corral gate and saw that, sure enough, a buckboard with one figure driving it, fast, was coming in across the sunset prairie and to hell with the bumps.

As Longarm got back to the dead wrangler sprawled near the gate, the buckboard driver reined to a stop nearby and he could see now that it was Mira Hecht from the coroner's office, clad in a canvas duster and a Stetson too big for her blonde head.

Longarm got to the buckboard first and doffed his own Stetson all the way before any of the others might be inspired to whistle at Miss Mira. This of course inspired all the hands to doff their own hats instead. The ramrod gruffly ordered one of the hands to see to the little lady's carriage horse. As Longarm helped her down, Mira snapped, "Norma Fraser's already been to my house to sign those papers. So what are you doing all the way out here?"

Longarm grinned sheepishly and replied, "Scouting up more business for your office, ma'am. If you were told I'd ridden out this way you must have been told why."

She turned from him to pick up the black bag she'd carried this far under her sprung seat as she said, trying not to smile, "We seem to have a busy season every time you pass through this otherwise peaceful county. How bad is it?"

"No more'n two cadavers for you to view. But I'd best warn you that what the scene may lack in numbers it makes up for in gore. You get to look at a cowboy and an Indian. You'd best look at the white boy first and save the Indian for later in the gathering dusk."

She glanced up at a sky now rose and lavender to say, "I could use more light right now." So the ramrod sent a hand to the bunkhouse for a lantern as Longarm led her to the dead wrangler with the others tagging along respectful.

Mira dropped to one knee by the body and opened her black bag to get out her notebook as she mused aloud, "Spine shot, from the seat of his jeans and the distance his hat flew. Wait, now. Why are these two entry wounds so packed with kindling?"

Longarm explained, "He was arrowed, not gunned, ma'am. I left both heads inside him, since there was no neat way to haul 'em out."

She sniffed, muttered, "Want to bet?" and slipped on

her red rubber gloves. Longarm knew what was coming next. So he didn't gasp like the others when she hauled out her cutlery and commenced to dig through shirt and hide and then some. Longarm had to allow she didn't mess him up any worse than she had to before she had two steel arrowheads from some trading post lined up on the dead man's shirt. Longarm started to say he'd already known most arrows came with heads. But on reflection they did seem to be forensic evidence. There were only a handful of older men who still had the time or even the know-how it took to knap a hunk of flint or jasper into a decent arrowhead. So he knew he didn't have to question any of those old-timers, while, at the same time he could see they'd been made for the Indian trade, not for the fancier archery sets some whites fooled about with. He told her, "I had an arrow from a fancy Eastern girl's school shot at me one time. Now all I have to know for certain is whether that other dead rascal was a real Indian, and I'll buy this as a brush with Indians until I find out better."

By this time the hand had returned with a bright coal-oil lantern. So Mira dropped the arrowheads in her black bag and got up with it, resisting an impulse to brush her dusty skirt with a bloody gloved hand.

One of the hands opened the gate for them, this time. Mira was unable to restrain a quickly choked-off gasp as she got her first look at the mangled as well as naked corpse trying to stare up at them by lantern light. A face with both eyes shot out didn't stare very well or all that pleasant. She said flatly, "I mean to declare the cause of this death multiple gunshot wounds with maybe a light-ning bolt thrown in. For I'd never have time to dig out all those rounds before decomposition set in. Remind me never to arrow a rider from *this* outfit."

Longarm said, "It might simplify your findings and comfort the dead wrangler's kin a mite if you just put down that the dead white likely killed the dead Indian, ma'am. I doubt there's room on one sheet of paper to list just everyone who gathered about to make sure this old boy was done for. The important question is whether he was *born* an Indian or just liked to dress unusual when he was raiding stock."

Mira dropped to her knee again and got out a bitty bottle and a big wad of cotton waste. As she wet the cotton and proceeded to rub it on a spot that wasn't all that torn up, the ramrod asked how come. Mira said, "If he stained his skin with anything that wouldn't kill him, earlier, it has to dissolve in chloroform. Could I have a bit more light, please? Not too close. Yes, that's just right. This stuff is sort of explosive."

She held the cotton waste up to the light. Even from where he stood, Longarm could see the cotton was just a mite greasy. She said as much. So he said, "We could still be talking about a bad breed or even a dark Mex. Is there any way to tell for certain, Miss Mira?"

She forced herself to gaze dispassionately at the busted up face of the dead man before she decided, "Lord knows what the shape of his skull might have been in life. But wait. If I could get a good look at a front tooth that hadn't been shattered by point-blank fire . . ."

"Want me to kick his teeth loose for you, ma'am?" asked the ramrod helpfully.

Mira thanked him for his laconic suggestion but said she'd rather do it her way. So as they watched with interest she got out her forceps and pulled a bicuspid the boys had somehow managed to miss. As she held the tooth up to the light she explained, "I had to pull this because it simply doesn't show from the front of a smile. Many Orientals and some but not all American Indians have front teeth indented this way down the rear surface. Folk of European or African ancestry never do. So this so-called shovel tooth reads pure Indian. Don't ask me what tribe."

Longarm said, "I'd guess at Algonquian if it mattered as much as a heap of suspects you've just eliminated, Miss Mira. From the little left of his body build, he was built in life a lot like us. Lakota are built more rawboned and Comanche or Kiowa tend to be more squatty."

One of the older Rocking Seven hands said, "Hold on. I never heard tell of no Algonquian in these parts."

To which Longarm replied, "Sure you have. Arapaho, Blackfeet, Cheyenne and even the army's Deleware scouts are all Algonquian at heart. We're a mite north for Arapaho and a mite south for Blackfeet. If some army Deleware have gone bad, this could really get confusing. So I'm betting on Cheyenne for now."

He lit a fresh smoke and, as he saw Mira rising back to her feet and closing her black bag, he held off on adding that the next question was which lodge they were talking about. She said she had some oilcloth sheeting in her buckboard but that she could use a little help in getting both bodies wrapped and up on the wagon bed. The ramrod told her to just stand back and let his boys handle the chore. But he added, "Are you fixing to take the dead redskin back to town as well, ma'am?"

She smiled demurely and said, "What did you have in mind, your woodpile? I have to go through some more motions on a zinc table before the county buries him, free, in Potter's Field. Anyone who wants to have a more formal funeral for your dead wrangler will have to wait until the coroner's jury releases his body as well."

So she got no more argument, even though more than one older hand opined that Sheridan County sure had gotten fancy in the past few years.

Once they had the assistant coroner back on her sprung seat with both bodies in the back and the reins in her once-more clean bare hands, Longarm untethered his own mount to carry her back to town in the cool shades of evening. It was almost as dark as it figured to get, by now, with the stars winking on overhead. Some of the Rocking Seven riders offered to tag along. But when Longarm told them he figured the Indians were long gone, and their ramrod told them they'd be riding out at dawn no matter what they felt like, Longarm got to escort the gal and her grim load solo.

As he walked his own mount at her side, Mira waited until they were well clear of the cattle spread before she asked, "Would you like to tell me, now, what you started to say back there about Indians and decided not to?"

He chuckled and said, "Remind me never to play poker with you, Miss Mira. I wasn't keeping no secrets. I just find it tedious to lecture cowboys on Indians or vice versa, since neither seem to want to know all that much about one another."

"I want to know. Just what do you think we have to worry about, Custis?"

He shrugged and said, "Worry might be putting it a mite strong for anyone safe in a town the size of Sheridan. If we were expecting a real Indian war you'd be talking to an army officer instead of a lawman right now. They only want me to see if I can find out how serious this recent hit-and-running might really be. I'd know a lot better if I could make that dead Indian in the back a Suicide Boy. All the reports so far have read Contrary Lodge. But that raid back to the Rocking Seven reads more Suicide Boy."

She said flatly, "Custis, I don't know what you're talking about."

So he explained, "Raiding stock in broad daylight and even getting caught, wearing no paint, reads a handful of young rascals inspired by the other troubles to see if they could make a coup to brag on. If that was all there was to it, your dead passenger's pals are doubtless feeling a might dumb right now. They rode out to steal ponies, authorized by nobody but the gals they bragged to, and now they have to explain how come they not only failed to lift one pony but left a dead comrade behind. It ain't true that Indians have no sense of humor. I hate to think of the mocking comments those old boys are facing, and I'm not even on their side."

She suggested, "They can boast that they killed a white man, can't they?"

But he shook his head and said, "Not the right way. According to their own religious notions, an enemy ain't really dead until you lift his hair and cut off his bow fingers. They do pick folk off at a distance. Everybody does. But they don't get to brag about it and their home folk would just as soon not sleep in the same lodge with 'em, after dark. You see, as they see it, a dead enemy left with his hair and unmutilated hands can make a mighty serious ghost. Cheyenne ghosts get to sneak about in the same condition they were left in. The Lakota don't worry about that as much. They say they're willing to take on a dead man they've already killed one time. Cheyenne are a heap more worried about cutting off fingers than taking scalps, though. So, like I said, the boys who ran off, leaving two powerful haunts behind, could be in a whole lot of trouble right now."

She thought before she spoke, unlike some. So they went on a piece before she said, "I can see why they'd be worried about the wrangler's ghost, with his gun hand still in fair shape. But why would the ghost of a dead Indian want to hurt his old friends, Custis?"

"For treating him unfriendly, of course. It's a Cheyenne sin to abandon a comrade to the enemy, even if you have to go down with him, trying. It makes some sense, once you buy a spirit world run along Man'tou lines. Wouldn't you be sore if you woke up dead to find your pals had run off to leave you wrapped in oilcloth in a white gal's buckboard, if you'd been brung up Cheyenne?"

She repressed a shudder and said, "Maybe I don't want to delve into Indian religion as much as I thought. I guess you have to, though, right?"

He nodded and said, "It's sort of interesting, even when it ain't useful to my job. But suffice it to say, those poor Suicide Boys have more to worry about than we do, right now."

Then somebody all too invisible in the darkness proved him all too wrong. Longarm tensed as he heard the hummingbird buzz of incoming arrows. Then Mira's draft horse screamed like a stuck pig, when they hit. As the mortally wounded horse fell to the sod between the shafts, Longarm had already scooped Mira from her buckboard seat and they were off and running, with her screaming more in surprise than anything else. Knowing they'd expect him to make a run for Sheridan to the south or the even closer Rocking Seven to the north, Longarm rode west, beelining for the Indian-haunted foothills in that direction. He hoped that might be the last way they'd be expecting him to ride. The pony under him and the girl proved its Morgan blood by covering a mile in less than four minutes. Then they were up on the Burlington railroad embankment. By this time Mira had stopped hollering and worked her shapely hips around to ride pillion behind him, sidesaddle, and clinging to him for dear life. He didn't want to stay skylined. So they were tearing down the far side before he spied a lonesome construction shack near a telegraph pole and made for it, grunting, "Just hang on a few more hops, honey. We may get to keep our hair after all!"

They did. Longarm hauled the panting pony into the empty shack after them. Then he shut the door, barred it from inside, and told Mira to hold the pony for a spell as he busted out all the window glass with the muzzle of his Winchester and fired the same, three times, before he turned back to her and said, "That ought to do it, for now. Whether the hands at the Rocking Seven respond to them distress shots or not, the rascals who just arrowed your horse have to worry that they might. So, like the old song says, farther along we'll know all about it. Are you hurt, seeing as we have time to talk, now?"

"I'm more shaken and confused than hurt. What on earth was that all about? Where are we, and why?"

He said, "I must know the sound of incoming arrows better than you, ma'am. I sure noticed we were getting hit by someone letting a mess of 'em fly. Once you've heard one horse take an arrow, mortal, you don't have to hang about and study on its possible injuries. It's time to run. So we did. As to this shack, I'd like to brag on how smart I was. But to tell the truth it was just here, praise the Lord and the Burlington railroad. They build these sheds every few miles along the line for the use of track walkers caught out on the range by unseasonable weather. Some of 'em have stoves, bunks and such. This one seems to be meant more for tools or real emergencies, depending. But that's all right. I doubt we'll be stuck here all that long and, if we are, I got a canteen of water and some canned beans and tomato preserves aboard my saddle. Could you use a drink?"

She said, "I surely could. But it wouldn't be water! What if they attack this shack? What if they set it afire around us?"

"We'll likely wind up dead," he said. "Meanwhile we have a six-gun and a Winchester to work with."

He drew his Colt Model T and handed it to her, saying, "I ain't out to insult your marksmanship, ma'am. It's only that I'm sharp as they come with a rifle and I mean to man the window facing the tracks while you watch the less likely far side. If they outline themselves against the Milky Way, coming over them higher tracks, I may be able to teach 'em better manners."

She gamely moved to the west window, but said, "I can't see a thing out this way and— Oh, I see, this is a double-action revolver, right?"

He moved to the pony, tethered it to a cross timber, gave it a reassuring pat on the muzzle and took up his own post at the east window, saying, "I should have told you that. Don't fool with the action until you're serious.

70

All you have to do is pull the trigger and it goes off easy as anything. That's how come I pack it."

He saw no reason to tell her about the wicked little vest-pocket derringer he'd only have to use if things came down to two last shots, which would hardly be wasted on Indians.

Chapter 5

A little over an hour later the quarter moon rose above the railroad bank. It had felt longer, and the moonlight wasn't all that bright. But at least any movement darker than the dry grass all about figured to be barely visible. Mira said, "I don't think anyone's out there."

"I don't think so, either. That's when you generally get killed. Nobody hardly ever breaks cover when they think someone's there."

She shifted her weight on her feet at her window and asked how long this frightening boredom was supposed to go on, adding that she was just dying to sit down, at least. He said, "They never built this fool shack with gazing out from a rocker in mind. I ain't all that comfortable, either. I've been studying a tumbleweed about twenty yards out. If I can't see it much clearer by the time the moon's risen some more, there may be a more comfortable way to manage. Meanwhile, let's just make sure none of them darker patches of darkness out there are creeping in on us."

She sighed and said, "I wouldn't be standing here on pins and needles if I wasn't watching out for night crawlers, darn it. How long is this supposed to go on?"

"I wish you wouldn't keep asking the same questions," he said. "If I was a mind reader I'd be making a lot more in show business than the infernal Justice Department sees fit to pay me now. If they were Suicide Boys out to recover that body they've had more than enough time to do so and head on home. If they were riding for the Contrary Lodge there's just no telling what they might have in mind right now. I suspect Contraries don't know their fool selves what they're supposed to do next."

She wrinkled her nose and said, "That really cheers me more than you can imagine. Don't they go by any rules at all?"

Longarm shrugged and said, "None they let any white man or even other Indians in on. You can't even count on 'em to always do the reverse of sensible. They work so hard at acting contrary that sometimes they act normal just to be contrary. The rascals are even more contrary than our own devil worshipers. White satanists start out half cracked to begin with. Indians who join the Contrary Lodge are sometimes sane as you or me."

She shifted her weight again and said, "I didn't know they were devil worshipers. I didn't even know the Indians had a devil."

"They call him, or them, Wendigo. Man'tou is the ramrod of the good spirits. Only they ain't got it worked out as formal as we have. The trouble with not having it all down in a Good Book is that every dream singer or medicine man has his own version, and the dream singers of the Contrary Lodge don't talk to nobody outside the lodge, see?"

"No," she answered. "How do you know so much about them if they never let outsiders in on their secret rules, Custis?"

Longarm was dying for a smoke. He fished out a cheroot to chew unlit and told her, "It ain't hard to figure the basic notion of a white demonist or an Indian Contrary, since they both have the same burr under their saddles. Folk don't turn their old-time religion inside out when things are going right and the spirit or spirits they were brung up to pray to seem to be treating 'em right. Back in the Middle Ages, when everyone in the old counties belonged to one church and life went on much the same day after day, nobody but the clergy worried all that much about the way the Lord seemed to be running things. So they just worked all week, went to church every Sabbath, and even their superstitions made some sense. Then they had the Black Death and their lords and masters started to nitpick and fight about the small print in the Good Book and things seemed to be going to hell in a hack no matter how you tried to please the Lord. So that's when a lot of folk took to devil worship, figuring that since the old rules failed 'em, *reversing* 'em might offer a better shake. I wasn't there. But from the little I've read about it, they acted sort of silly and disgusting. They said the Lord's Prayer backwards, busted the Ten Commandments even when it wasn't any fun, and put their trust in crazy old ladies squatting in the woods instead of the bishop in the cathedral who couldn't seem able to stop the plague or make the landlord behave his fool self."

She said, "Heavens, you surely must read a lot. But what has white witchcraft or satanism got to do with these weird Indians of yours, Custis?"

"They ain't mine. They think Man'tou has turned his back on them, too. Things have gone sour on 'em since they were free and proud with all this range to themselves. None of the chants and ceremonies they lived by did them a lick of good as they got licked in battle after battle with our kind. So in more recent times an Indian or more has taken to thinking like some of our kind did when they couldn't get the Good Book to work and hadn't studied on science, yet. They've got that pesky Wovoka preaching his Ghost Dance Religion, other medicine men chawing cactus dope in hopes of coming up with *some* damn vision that can get the B.I.A. off their backs, and of course the Contrary Lodge acting even crazier, acting like mean little kids who sass all their elders. They say that when Tatanka-yatanka was holding a war council with Red Cloud and the other chiefs one time, a fool Contrary slapped the old medicine man across the face with a sweaty breechclout and stormed out to lead a raid against a nation the Lakota were at peace with. So, naturally, now that all the main chiefs are at peace with us ... keep your pretty eyes peeled and let's hope those were Suicide Boys."

She sighed and said, "My eyes are the least of my problems. I don't see how I'm ever going to stay on my poor *feet* all night!"

Longarm thought a spell about that. The dark blur of tumbleweed looked just about the same out there as the sliver of moon rose ever higher. He said, "Yeah, there has to be a better way. Why don't you spread my bedroll as far from that pony as you can manage and just crawl between the blankets for now?"

She gasped and said, "I *beg* your pardon!"

"I meant alone, of course. I'm going up on the roof. It offers a better field of fire for me alone than the two of us have at this level. I doubt anyone will notice me as more than a blob up there, even if they expect to see me in such a ridiculous position."

She heaved a sigh of relief and said, "Oh, I thought—"

"You thought mighty little of my brains, then," he

cut in. "No offense, but even if you were willing, you just ain't pretty enough to die in bed with. Bar the door after me and see if you can find a bucket, a box, or whatever to give the pony some canned beans and tomato preserves before you turn in. He won't need canteen water with tomato juice. So save it for us."

She laughed wildly and said, "You can't be serious! Who ever heard of feeding beans and tomatoes to a horse?"

"Me. We don't have no oats. Ponies are vegetarians, ain't they? Concentrated vegetables ought to make up for the short rations, and anyone can see there's no grass growing in here. I'm going out and up now. You'd best hang on to my pistol, and here's a fistful of extra rounds. Make sure you put one aside as a last resort if things go sour."

Then he eased the door open, slipped outside, and moved around to the west side, away from the tracks and anyone taking cover behind the bank of the same. He tossed the Winchester up on the flat roof and followed it, using the windowsill as a ladder rung as he grabbed the edge of the roof in both hands.

Once he was sprawled atop the shed, Winchester back in his hands and aimed at the railroad bank, he felt sort of dumb for waiting this long. For he had a fine field of fire in every direction. He could even see the open prairie on the far side of the railroad some, and unless they'd been smart enough to leave their ponies farther out this time, there didn't seem to be anyone menacing them as far as he could see all around.

He couldn't see all that *far*, of course. But it was surely starting to look as if they'd outrun a simple hit-and-run. If the attack had been an attempt to recover that dead Indian, it could be over. Trying to think contrary to the usual rules of Indian fighting, he wondered whether Contraries would try anything as sensible as saving a dead pard's remains, cutting up the remains of the dead wrangler, and either ride off or try to move in. He told himself to stop running his brain in circles and just wait and see. That didn't sound too interesting, either.

He muttered softly, "I sure hate warfare, civilized or uncivilized. When you ain't getting killed it can get tedious as hell!"

As if in answer, he heard the door under him creak open, and Mira called out in a little-girl voice, "Custis, I'm scared to death down here by myself."

He said, "Well of course you're scared. You'd be loco en la cabeza if you wasn't. You'd still be better off in that old bedroll. It figures to get colder before it gets warmer, tonight."

She pleaded, "Can't I come up there with you?"

So he thought about that. Then he decided, "I don't see why not, if you enjoy fresh air more than I do. It's already getting sort of nippy up here and the night's still young."

She replied by throwing the bedroll up on the roof. Longarm put the Winchester aside and reached down to grab one of her hands and haul her up and over the edge. As she rolled away from the drop she said, "My, you're strong." Then she shivered inside her duster and added, "You're right. It does seem a lot colder up here. What if we spread the bedroll and sort of got in it together to keep warm? Could I trust you?"

He chuckled and said, "Nope. But you go on and get a blanket and tarp between the west wind and your thinclad hide whilst I stand watch. The only time I admire this suit my boss makes me wear is when it gets a mite cool for jeans."

So as he peered about with his Winchester at nothing much, she spread the bedding atop the flat roof and got in it. He noticed, from the corner of his eye, that she'd shucked her duster, and was that a print summer dress she'd tossed atop her hat and duster? He decided that seemed fair, since he'd said he meant to keep watch *outside* the bedding. Just thinking about that made him feel colder as a gust of wind off the mountains tried to crawl up his pant legs. As if she'd read his mind, Mira asked, "Aren't you just freezing out there, Custis? I didn't know how many goose bumps I'd been growing until I got inside these nice warm blankets. And you can point your gun just as good from in here with me, can't you?"

He growled, "This Winchester might not be the only thing I wound up pointing unless some damned Indians arrived in time to save your virtue. For Pete's sake, Mira, you must have some medical training to go with your job. Don't you know nothing about human anatomy? The kind as goes with *live* folk, I mean?"

She giggled and said, "I know what you mean. They taught us about that in medical school. I wasn't sure I believed it until just now. But it does seem true that being scared skinny makes a body feel sort of, well, sexually aroused. Why do you suppose that is?"

He shrugged and said, "Beats me. I've always been able to get horny whether I was scared or not."

She sighed and said, "Speak for yourself. I usually seem to feel prim and proper, save when I'm alone in bed and wondering why I went and said no again. But for some reason, ever since I started wondering if I'd ever see the sun rise again, I've been getting hotter for a man between my thighs by the minute! Do you think that's so awful? Am I shocking you?"

He chuckled and said, "Not hardly. But do I have your promise you'll respect me in the morning?"

She laughed wickedly and said, "Oh, get in here with me, you bashful thing."

So he did. But then, being a woman, Mira naturally decided she'd just been funning as soon as he started loving her up with the Winchester handy, near their heads, just in case. He'd met her kind before. Every man who wasn't a sissy likely had. Unlike most men she'd likely pulled this faint-hearted act on, Longarm knew how to deal with such bullshit. He knew that no matter what Don Juan and Casanova had bragged, there was simply no way, short of punching a gal in the jaw, to uncross her fool legs until she just couldn't stand to keep 'em crossed anymore. So he let go and rolled belly-down atop his erection, thankful he still he had pants and undershirt on, and propped himself up on his elbows for another look around.

She gasped, "Oh, what's wrong? Do you see anything, dear?"

He replied in a not unfriendly tone, "Nope. But it pays to see them before they see us."

"Oh, I thought something was wrong when you just gave up like that, so suddenly."

He told her soothingly, "It's all right, honey. Why don't you try for some shut-eye?"

"At a time like this?" she demanded. "You *touched* me! You actually had your fingers in me, just now!"

"I noticed," he said. "You sure have a nice little love-box. But seeing as you don't want to share it with nobody, why don't we just forget all about it?"

She murmured, "Oh, I've made you angry! I swear I

79

didn't want to upset you, Custis. I was *trying* to respond to you, just now, but it's been so long since I've really been wicked, and I hardly know you, and I'm so confused about all this and—"

"I said not to worry about it," he cut in, trying not to screw the roof under his raging hard-on. "I'm not sore. You got a right to feel confused. I'm just a stranger riding through and you'd be dumb to go all the way with a man like me. My job calls for me to tumbleweed more than I might like to, and the only thing I have to offer any poor gal is some free and easy no-strings loving with the assurance I never kiss and tell. You'd best save your virginity for some old Sheridan gent who'll hang about under your window for a spell afterwards."

She didn't answer for a time. Then she said softly, "I lost my virginity back East, in school, for which I've ever been sort of grateful. As to having lovers mooning about the quarters of an unmarried lady in a small town, that's the main reason I'm so out of practice, damn it!"

He chuckled and said, "Yeah, small-town gossip is really something, even if Queen Victoria does live clean across the ocean. I can see why you'd have to worry so about your reputation in town. It was sure smart of you to stop me before you could get in trouble."

She frowned and asked, "What trouble are you talking about? I happen to be a trained nurse and I'd be a doctor if they'd treated us girls decent at graduation."

He lay flatter beside her but made no further move as he assured her, "I know most gals with any sense know how to take care of themselves. I was speaking of your reputation in town."

"Damn it," she said, "we're not *in* town right now, are we?" So he decided it was worth another try and, this time, as he got to playing with her some more, she

80

spread her legs wide, even as she sobbed, "Oh, Custis, what are you *doing* to me?"

He thought that was a dumb question. So he didn't try to answer her in words. He just whipped out his old organ grinder and rolled aboard to put it where they both thought it really belonged. As she felt him entering her, Mira gasped and pleaded, "Wait, it's too big and I'm not sure we really should and . . . don't you want to take your pants off, now, for heaven's sake?"

He did. It wasn't easy, leaving it inside her as he undressed under the covers. But he didn't want to start with her from scratch, even bare-ass, and she seemed to be one of those gals who expected a damn-fool approach to good old down-home slap-and-tickle. But once he'd made her climax, fast, she seemed to feel more willing to let herself go. She got so willing, in fact, that they both wound up with bruises from bouncing all over that hard old roof most of the night. He didn't dare go to sleep, and Mira didn't seem to want to until the sun came up to catch them at it, dog style. Then he figured it was safe to head for town.

Longarm thought it only natural that a man and woman riding into town aboard one pony rated some polite but curious stares. But Longarm didn't dwell in Sheridan. As she clung to his waist whether she still wanted to or not, Mira murmured, "Oh, Custis, I feel so low-down and ashamed. I can't believe we did all those awful things back there last night!"

He asked, "Did we do something awful? That's funny. All I seem to recall is that we spent the night forted up with this pony as a sort of chaperone, surrounded by Indians."

That cheered her some, but her voice was still subdued as she got him to promise, more than once, that he'd never, ever, tell anyone she'd even kissed him, let alone where she'd wound up kissing him when he'd had trouble getting it up that last time or two.

When they got to her house she made him wait out on the porch so he could sign her coroner's report in plain view of all her neighbors. When he'd done so and asked when, if ever, she wanted him to drop by again, she sighed and said, "It's over between us, Custis. Please try not to shoot anyone else before you leave town. I know it was as much my fault as yours, but I don't think we ought to see one another anymore."

He nodded, said he understood, and turned to go. But as he did so she plucked at his sleeve to stop him and murmured, "I don't want you to turn around. I have to be strong. But I want you to know I'll never forget you. It was lovely, even though I never want to see you again."

He'd already said he understood. So he just kept walking. Then he mounted the cordovan and rode it back to the livery. He told the colored stable hands they'd been right about those Morgan lines, tipped them handsomely once they'd saddled up his Indian Agency bay, and headed out again to do some more riding, now that he'd seen Mira safely home.

But as he passed the lockup the young deputy hailed him from the doorway. So he dismounted to see what was up. The town law told him, "If you was going back for the coroner's meat wagon, it's parked over by the morgue. Some Rocking Seven riders just brung it into town. You just missed 'em. They say they found it near sunup with even its draft horse dead. Somebody stole a dead Indian and cut up that dead white boy in the back as well."

Longarm hauled out a couple of cheroots, handed one to the kid, and got them both to smoking as he said, "Saves me a trip. Any word on that local posse yet?"

The town law said, "Yep. Come on inside. Got a mess of wires to show you. One is for you, from your Denver office. I didn't think you'd mind if I brung it along, as long as I never opened it."

Longarm smiled thinly and said that saved him another trip. On the desk inside lay all the yellow Western Union envelopes in question. The deputy took the chair and Longarm hooked a rump over one corner of the desk as they read the wires. Longarm was cussing some before they were done.

For the sheriff and his posse were clear up the line in or about the whistle stop at Parkman by now. They'd loaded their mounts aboard freight cars down near Cedar Creek and circled farther but faster by rail to do something about an Indian raid up that way. But meanwhile, according to Billy Vail, a mess of *other* Indians painted and acting contrary had hit a cow spread to the southeast, in Campbell County, and so Longarm's new orders were to forget the foolishness and come on home.

Longarm told the Sheridan deputy, "Sometimes my boss makes sense. They're handing it over to the War Department. There's just no way one band could be hitting in so many places. The chiefs are all denying they want another war with us. But neither the Justice Department, the B.I.A., nor I knows what to call war bands hitting all over creation if it ain't at least a modest war."

The town law looked worried and said, "I sure wish you didn't have to leave so soon."

To which Longarm replied with a fatalistic shrug,

"Me too. I feel sort of sorry for old Little Wolf's band. I'm pretty sure he doesn't have any Contraries sheltering with him. But he is sort of surly, and there is a renegade charge outstanding against those particular Cheyenne. So I fear the army will simply commence the festivities with long-range Hotchkiss fire. I was hoping I could nip the trouble in the bud. But, so far, I haven't been able to get one Indian around here to do one thing but grab for my hair."

He knew what Dancing Moon had grabbed for, first, didn't cut much ice with the U.S. Cav, even if he had been a kiss and tell. He could only hope they'd miss her entire or kill her clean when they lobbed those shells across the Tongue.

The young deputy asked how soon Longarm thought the army might take to get there. Longarm said he didn't know, explaining, "With President Hayes busting a gut to balance the budget, many an officer might hesitate to take the field before someone can tell him where replacements and fresh ammo might be coming from. On the other hand, some old boys put glory and possible promotion ahead of any other consideration. So figure any time from right now to next month and you're as likely as me to be right."

The junior lawman did, looked unhappy, and said, "I sure wish you'd see fit to stick around until that posse got back, at least. I'm stuck here with just this one official badge and a handful of part-time beat walkers until that fool sheriff brings back all the real lawmen we have in these parts."

Longarm shrugged and said, "I noticed that when the Clifford boys were robbing your bank. It's a hell of a way to run a town half this size. But it wasn't us old boys from the Justice Department as drug almost all the township and county law off to play hide-and-seek with maybe half that many Indians, and we do have other fish to fry."

He took a thoughtful drag on his cheroot and added, "I got me some things as need to be done here in Sheridan before I give it back to you and the coal miners entire. My railroad timetable tells me there's a late-night train that'll take me back to Denver with fewer stops and changes than the one as leaves this noon. That gives me time to figure a way I can return an Indian Agency pony without riding it all the way to Montana, take me a bath, and catch me some sleep, in that order. So you'll likely find me at the Richardson Livery or the Pronghorn Hotel if you need me, unless I'm at the Western Union or . . . never mind. If there's any more shooting in town before I have to leave, I'll likely notice."

He headed for the door. The young deputy rose to tag along, as if that might convince Longarm he shouldn't follow the orders of Billy Vail. A lot of times, Longarm received orders that made him sort of pensive. But he always followed orders when they made a lick of sense, and anyone could see this Indian trouble had grown all out of proportion for any one man to cope with.

As if to prove that, the two lawmen heard a mess of wild war whoops coming down the street as they stepped out into the same. The town law drew his gun. Longarm saw no need to as they both gazed north at the oncoming riders. Cowhands hardly ever rode into town whooping and laughing to rob a bank.

There were nine of them in all, with what seemed to be a captive Indian they'd brought in with his hands bound to the horn of the stock saddle he was sitting, in his fringed buckskin shirt and old faded army pants. He wore no feathers or paint. The black braids hanging down to frame his brown moon face were frosted with gray. The face itself wore an expression midway between that of a good poker player and a gent who'd just stepped in shit. One of the cowhands called out to them, "Look what we catched out on the prairie this morning. We brung him into town to hang, no trees being handy and him not putting up no fight. Is that posse back yet, Slim?"

The young town deputy said, "Nope. Lord knows when it will be. But I reckon I can handle one old Sioux 'til they wander home."

Then, to his credit, he asked, "What makes you all think this old boy was on the warpath? No offense, but if he was riding all alone, in boots and pants on a stock saddle, with no face paint . . ."

By now the Indian was staring at Longarm with an expression of total disgust. So, since Longarm was having a time keeping his own face half that straight, he grinned and called out, "Howdy, Laughing Raven. How did you ever manage to get captured by these old boys who can't seem to tell a Crow from a Lakota?"

As the captors frowned in wonder the captive growled, "I call my enemies Sioux, too. Hear me. I was not expecting Americans to jump me as I brewed my coffee. If I had, they would not have known I was in that draw just off a public trail!"

One of the hands who'd brought Laughing Raven in asked the town law if they knew who Longarm was. When they learned he was the famous Longarm, they looked down at him from their mounts a lot less scowly. But one of them demanded, "Who's this redskin if you think you know him, Marshal Long?"

Longarm said, "I'm only a deputy marshal and I

don't *think* I know Laughing Raven. I can tell you for certain he's the chief of police at the Crow Agency, just a ways off." Then he asked the older Indian lawman, "How come you were riding out of uniform during a time of Indian trouble, and how come you didn't tell these boys who you were, you muley old cuss?"

Laughing Raven shrugged and said, "I don't think even a rider of the Sparrow Hawk People could get very close to a Contrary war party wearing government blue and a pewter badge. I tried to tell these young men I was on their side. But every time I tried to open my mouth someone punched me in the face. I was headed this way, anyhow. Wa, I am here. I wish someone would untie me."

That sounded reasonable to Longarm as well. But since there always had to be an asshole or more in any crowd of uneducated country boys, a heavyset hand with brows that met in the middle snapped, "Hold on, now. We catched this old Sioux way the hell off any reservation and I, for one, never heard tell of anything as unusual sounding as an Indian police chief, damn it!"

Longarm tried to recall what the Good Book said about a soft answer turning away wrath as he replied, "You must know more about cows than the U.S. government, then. To begin with, since any Indian's word is worth about as much as that of any white boy you don't know personal, and since Indians work cheaper, Uncle Sam has even Apache on his payroll as official lawmen, army scouts and such. In the second place, Laughing Raven, here, is what we folk call a Crow. The Crow, Pawnee, Western Deleware and such are on our side against the ferocious Lakota Confederacy even when they *ain't* on the government payroll. They don't cotton to losing their scalps and ponies any more than we do. So why don't somebody cut this old boy's hands free before we wind up with yet another nation mad at us, damn it?"

The beetle-browed hand did no such thing. But a smarter looking rider swung his mount closer to Laughing Raven's and started to carve away the rawhide thongs, saying, "I recall my old uncle who liked to trap beavers saying Crow was decent enough if you treated 'em polite. I'm sorry if we misjudged you, Chief. But you see how we thought we was doing the right thing, don't you?"

Laughing Raven raised his freed wrists to rub some life back into them as he replied grudgingly, "You people have always been real assholes about us. Those Contrary raiders must be assholes, too. I would like to have my guns back, now."

A sheepishly smiling rider handed the older Indian a repeating Remington rifle as another wistfully returned a handsome pair of ivory handled army-issue revolvers, saying, "We figured you might have picked these up at Little Big Born, seeing it ain't all that far from here in time or distance."

Laughing Raven shoved the rifle in its saddle boot and then strapped on his six-guns, saying, "These guns *were* taken from the body of one of Custer's officers. I took them from the Lakota who won them in battle. The battle *we* had was a good one, too. My heart soars when I think of the medicine such guns must have by now. As we talked while he lay dying, the Lakota, who'd fought well, told me the soldier he'd taken them from had been a brave fighter, too."

One of the cowhands observed some might feel

spooked at the ownership of weaponry with such an unlucky history. Laughing Raven shrugged, made an unflattering observation about men who were afraid of Brother Owl, as the Crow referred to death, and got down stiffly to face Longarm and say, "Wa, first we drink some firewater and then we go after those Contraries. We are both great trackers. Nobody else around here could read the sign of a rabbit from that of a fox, in deep snow. But the two of us, hunting together—"

"It's too late," Longarm cut in, explaining, "the army's been called in and I've been called back to Denver, pard. But as long as you're here, I do have an agency pony you might want to carry back north with you."

Laughing Raven scowled and demanded, "Do I look like a damned pony wrangler? Hear me! When we heard of the trouble at the Crow Agency I asked permission, and got it, to see if I could cut the trail of those painted assholes before someone got hurt. I don't *want* the damned army hunting anybody around here! They recruit children just off the boat from across the great bitter water and when they're not getting lost out here they seem to think a cow bird or an antelope is an enemy rider. The army shoots at everybody, of every nation, and even though they miss most of the time, it makes our women and children cry. How soon do your orders say you have to go back to Denver, damn it?"

Longarm thought. Then he said, "Billy Vail only told me to give it up and come on back. He never said exactly when. I reckon I can hang about at least until the army shows up."

Laughing Raven grinned and said, "Wa, let's go get

that drink. Maybe the spirits will give us a good vision."

Longarm knew that under federal law a reservation Indian wasn't supposed to be served the sort of spirits that came in bottles. On the other hand, they weren't on any pesky reservation. So he just nodded and invited all the other boys to come along as well.

Chapter 6

But, even sticking with draft suds, Longarm was having a tough time keeping his red-rimmed eyes open by the time Laughing Raven had gotten jake with the other whites in town. The young town lawman had said his red fellow peace officer was welcome to bed down in an unlocked cell at the town lockup if and when he ever got tired enough to lie down. So Longarm told Laughing Raven to try and stay sober, catch some shut-eye before sundown, and that they'd meet again just before moonrise to see about some serious night riding.

Then he led his pony back to the livery, told it the same thing, and headed for the hotel he'd decided on. But as he passed the gun shop of Miss Norma he decided to tie up a possible loose end, first. He entered to find her serving a customer and waited until the gent left with his new shotgun. As soon as they were alone, the pretty little widow grinned at him and gushed, "Oh, Custis, how can I ever thank you? I've made four sales and it isn't noon yet!" Then she shot him a keener look across the counter and demanded, "What's wrong with you, dear heart? You look as if the dogs have had you under the back porch!"

He smiled wanly and said, "I could use a good tub soak and a few hours' sleep, in that order. But I reckon I can get both at the Pronghorn up the street. What I came here for was to ask if you sold archery stuff, like steel arrowheads, as well as guns and ammunition."

She looked sincerely surprised and replied, "Good heavens. I've never had any call for *Indian* ammunition, Custis. Don't they sell those manufactured arrowheads at Indian trading posts and such?"

He nodded but said, "To trade at a licensed reservation post you got to be a reservation Indian. The only unreconstructed redskins I know of in these parts escaped from Fort Reno over a year ago. If Little Wolf's band have had any luck at all with foothill deer and elk, they ought to be using old-time arrows by this time. Those Contraries I told you about are still using steel tips, too freely and too accurately for comfort. It does make one wonder, doesn't it?"

She said, "I see what you mean. Maybe some Indian trader on a nearby reservation has had a run on arrowheads he may have been smart enough to record for you. Nobody here in town trades all that much with Indians. Why on earth would anyone want to?"

Longarm sighed wearily and said, "Asking a heap of damn-fool questions goes with this job, ma'am. Even when the answer to a question is just what you might expect, it's an answer. I got to get on over to the hotel now, before my fool legs give out under me entire."

But she came around the counter to block his exit as she told him firmly, "You're in no condition to go anywhere, and besides, they charge extra for a hot bath at the Pronghorn. Why don't you just stay here with me? It'll only take a few minutes to draw you a hot bath and I just changed my sheets this morning."

Longarm gulped and said, "That's surely a tempting offer. But to tell the truth, I can't say I'd be man enough, this side of a few hours' worth of shut-eye."

She blushed like a rose and said, "Don't talk dirty. We both know I have to stay out front and tend to business, thanks to the fame and fortune you brought into my life, you big goof."

He smiled down at her sheepishly and started to say he didn't want to be such a bother. But as he thought of walking even as far as the hotel under a hot autumn sun, and then no doubt arguing about a room and bath at such short notice, he told her he was willing if she was. So a few minutes later he lay wet and naked in a lion's paw cast-iron tub full of hot water, trying not to fall asleep and drown before he soaked his hide free of a lot of trail dust and a little of Mira Hecht. Old Norma had snuck some perfumed bath salts into the tub as she'd filled it for him.

Once he felt clean he let the stink-pretty out and used fresh tap water and a rag to rinse most of the stink-pretty off. But he still felt like a flower bed as he dried off with a luxurious turkish towel she'd left there for him. The fool woman kept her linen closet reeking of lavender as well.

She'd showed him where the one bedroom was before she'd headed back out front. So he just scooped up his stuff and ducked out bare-assed in hopes he might not meet her in the dinky back hallway of her combined shop and quarters.

He did. She gasped and almost dropped the terry-cloth robe she was holding as he quickly covered his naked privates with his hat and dangling boots and gun rig. She said, "Oh, I'm sorry. I was about to leave this old robe of my late husband's on the doorknob for you."

"Oh, that's all right, ma'am. I'm halfway there by now." She replied with a thoughtful little faraway smile,

"Silly me. I don't think a man your size could fit into this normal-sized robe to begin with."

Then she turned and headed back out front, the exposed flesh of her neck, below her upswept hair, at least as red as Longarm felt he was blushing as he turned his bare ass on her and ducked into the cozy sweet-scented bedroom.

He threw everything but the gun rig wherever it had a mind to wind up. Then he hung his six-gun on a bedpost and slid between the freshly starched and lavendered sheets. It felt as if he was a big old bee bedding down in a flower. He had no idea why it was giving him a hard-on. So he just closed his eyes as his head hit a pair of pillows as soft and smooth as breasts, and the next thing he knew he seemed to be tied to a stake near a camp fire while a mess of Indians painted all sorts of crazy colors danced around him. They didn't seem to notice he had no clothes on. But it made him feel silly, just the same. He tried to recall how in thunder he could have gotten into this fix. He'd never yet ridden into an Indian camp bare-assed. He asked Dancing Moon what was up when she danced over to him, wearing nothing but red and white stripes like a bawdy barber's pole. She said, "Hear me. We are going to burn you at the stake. But I am contrary. So I love you and I want to please you before I lift your hair!"

She sure knew how to pleasure a man's privates with her soft gentle hand. It felt mighty embarrassing as she got it all the way up for him in the middle of a war dance. But none of the others seemed to be paying any attention as the teasing little squaw sank to her knees in front of him and proceeded to puff on his old peace pipe. He knew he was fixing to come in her hot and sassy mouth any second. So he told her not to waste it and let him come in her right. She giggled and shoved him over backwards, stake and all, to fork a barber-striped thigh across him and impale her sweet self on his raging erection, asking him if he liked it better that way. He said he sure did and then his hands were somehow loose and he was hugging her down against him as she bounced just right and . . . how come she was suddenly wearing a silk chemise, and the camp fire was commencing to look more like sunset through lace curtains, and where had all the Indians gone?

He decided, "I must be having me a wet dream," even as he rolled Dancing Moon on her back to finish in her, right before he could wake up.

He knew he was going to damn it wake up before he could come all the way. But, then, to his surprise, he was awake, and still coming, as Dancing Moon turned into Norma Fraser and she was moving in time with him just right, crooning, "Oh, yess, don't stop! Don't ever stop! Just keep doing it and doing it until I die and go all the way to heaven!"

As Longarm shook his head to clear it, he kept moving in her love-slicked little organ grinder, if only because he couldn't come up with a thing to say that might not sound awkward as hell. He saw, now, that he'd mistaken a proper white lady for a bawdy red one in the process of awakening from a sort of nice nightmare. But she didn't seem to mind as he kept trying for a second shot into such a warm, wet little bull's-eye. She seemed to be trying to help his aim as she bounced in time with his thrusts, as a matter of fact. So he spread her stocking-clad legs as wide as he could and tried to hit bottom as she gasped, "Oh, Jesus, you're killing me and I just love it!"

He figured that had to be true by the time they'd

wound up on the rug, with her chemise removed entire and her squatting atop him again, sobbing mindlessly as she tossed her now unbound hair from side to side as they climaxed in mighty friendly unison.

Then she suddenly fell limp atop him and commenced to weep all over his naked chest as he held her in his arms. He told her he didn't see what either of 'em had to cry about. But she said, "Oh, Custis, whatever must you think of me? I swear I didn't mean to take advantage of you like this. But when I tiptoed in to awaken you at sunset, as you'd asked, you'd kicked the top sheet down, and you had such a grand erection as you lay there with such a sweet expression that I . . . I guess I went sort of crazy. I've been sleeping alone so long, and you have such a lovely body and I only meant to sort of touch you, but . . ."

He kissed the part of her hair and thrust his hips gently as he assured her, "I forgive you, honey. It was a grand way to wake up."

She moved her head up to kiss him full on the lips with a gasp of pleased wonder before she said, "Good heavens, you're still in me, hard! Don't you ever get enough, darling?"

He said, honestly enough, "It depends on where it's at. You sure fit me snugly, little darling."

She clamped down harder with her love-starved innards, saying, "I know. As I stood there in the doorway, gazing down at all you had to offer in the sunset's rosy glow, I just had to know what it felt like to take that much, or try to. I was afraid you might be too big for me. I told myself not to try. And then the next thing I knew I had and, oh, doesn't it seem as if we were just tailor-made for one another, darling?"

He glanced at the ever darkening light through her

lace curtain as he replied, "You couldn't have been made to my measure one stitch better, either way, by a Boston glove maker. But I did ask you to wake me up at sundown with other chores in mind."

She sighed and said, "I know. But couldn't we do it one more time before you leave, darling?"

He told her that was like asking a mean little kid if he was up to throwing one more rock at a greenhouse. But since he was running low on time he braced her on her hands and knees atop the bed to enter her, standing, from behind. She protested at first that she'd never before done it in such an undignified position. But then, like most gals discovering there was always a first time, she arched her spine and thrust her perky bare rump up to take him deeper and confided that there was a lot to be said for the way critters did it, after all. He didn't have time to get into Professor Darwin's notions about folk being natural critters long before they'd stood up and put on duds. So he just brought her to climax, fast, fired the last of his own ammo into her, and allowed, wistfully, it was time to go hunting less attractive asses.

As he wiped himself dry with a sheet corner and started to get dressed, Norma lay sprawled across the bed in just her stockings, regarding him with mixed emotions. She said, "Making love with you could get to be a habit, Custis. But you won't tell anyone, will you?"

He hauled on a boot as he chuckled and replied, "I was brung up not to brag. So I can't. Nobody would ever believe an ugly old cuss like me could wind up kissing more than the hand of such a fairy-tale princess as you."

She dimpled and said, "Liar. You know you're a Greek god and no man ever learned to move in a woman

97

like that without a lot of practice. I guess you get a lot of loving everywhere you wander, right?"

He hauled on the other boot as he told her sincerely, "Not in the sort of places I may wind up tonight, if Laughing Raven and me ain't careful. I was having a mighty odd dream about members of the Contrary Lodge just before you made my dreams come true. But I somehow doubt any rascals who get the drop on me in real life will treat me half that friendly."

He got to his feet and was strapping on his gun before he shifted his weight experimentally and added, "Damn. That last all-too-tempting quickie is going to call for a heap of black coffee, you cruel sweet-built little thing!"

Longarm found Laughing Raven awake and reading reward posters at the town lockup. The Indian lawman said, "Hear me. Your young men have less heart than ours. They only seem interested in money, women, or personal revenge. Don't they ever do anything crazy just because their visions tell them to?"

Longarm said, "Oh, we got lots of crazy folk, pard. But seeing we don't hold with lunatics having powerful medicine, we keep 'em in asylums instead of in prison with the just plain ornery."

Then, since first things generally came first and they could be facing a long night on the trail, Longarm hauled Laughing Raven off to the beanery near the rail stop where the grub was good as well as cheap. The Greek who ran the place raised a bushy brow at Longarm's even swarthier sidekick and allowed he didn't serve Indians. But he relented when Longarm assured him neither of 'em wanted to eat an Indian, but that they just might wreck the place if they didn't eat *something*, damned sudden.

As the Greek muttered over his fry plate with his broad ass turned to them, Longarm confided to Laughing Raven, "I dunno. A gal who said she surely liked me was just saying I reminded her of a Greek . . . god. I hope she was referring to the kind as posed for all them marble statues. I've seen live Greeks both pretty and ugly as that one. But I've never yet met one as ran about naked except for a maple leaf and a fireman's helmet, have you?"

Laughing Raven observed, "All you Americans look about the same to us, unless you happen to be black or Chinee. Some Chinee look almost normal, to us. But why are we talking of funny looking Americans? I thought we were after Contrary riders, most likely Cheyenne."

Longarm nodded but said, "Everybody sure seems to suspect 'em as Cheyenne. Little Wolf told me personal his band ain't got no Contrary Lodge. Of course, he tried to have me killed, right after. But it ain't such a big band, and when Little Wolf busted out from Fort Reno with Dull Knife that time, they didn't seem to have no Contraries riding with 'em. Save for scaring the liver and lights out of everyone paler faced than me and thee, the Cheyenne Autumn of seventy-eight was about as friendly as Indian troubles ever get. Dull Knife led his band, mostly women and children, through at least five hundred miles of fairly settled country without lifting one scalp or even winging anyone who wasn't pressing him too close for his comfort. They had many a crack at many a lonesome homestead or lightly manned cow spread as they pushed on for their old hunting grounds on the north range. Many a white who watched them pass had reason to feel grateful, after he or she got to breathe more regular, that Dull Knife acted more homesick than ferocious."

The Greek brought their blue-plate specials and coffee to them before Laughing Raven could reply. The big Crow looked warily down at his serving and decided, "Wa, meat and potatoes stick to a rider's backbone. But what are these greasy green worms doing on my plate?"

"They're called string beans," Longarm explained. "I don't like 'em either. But you always get roast beef, mashed potatoes and string beans off a Greek cook. I suspect that in cow country they get to serve the string beans over and over. But it's a sort of Greek custom, like them firemen's helmets some of 'em wear."

He smiled pleasantly at the bemused Greek behind the counter and said, "We're going to want plenty of coffee, with and after. I take mine black. My pard, here likes flour instead of sugar to put in his. What kind of pie do you have for dessert?"

The Greek shrugged and answered, "Two kinds appelous. Appelous and pine-appelous, five cents extra. Make that two bits and you get to fuck the diss-washer."

Longarm suspected the Greek had been out west longer than he let on. He laughed and said he was sorry for talking so mean about the string beans. But, just the same, neither he nor Laughing Raven touched the infernal rabbit grub.

As the Greek delivered a tin sifter and watched in utter dismay, Laughing Raven floured his coffee to his own taste and told Longarm, "Dull Knife was not looking for a fight. He got one at White River, just the same, but you were right about him only wanting to go home to the hunting grounds he knew. Little Wolf served under Dull Knife as head of the Crooked Lances.

That is why he and some of the better fighters got away at White River. I don't think Little Wolf was ever a Contrary. The medicine of the two lodges is very different. But look what I found, just before those cowboys jumped me between here and Parkman, the last place hit by those Contraries."

He reached inside his fringed jacket and deposited two tiny dots on the counter between their plates. Longarm put them in a spoon and held them up to the light before he nodded and said, "Blue wampum, likely scraped off a moccasin. You say you *spotted* these, in prairie grass, from aboard your pony?"

Laughing Raven shrugged modestly and said, "It was daylight. I was *looking* for sign. They are not wampum. They are made of glass in an Italian place called Venice for the Indian traders. But they are blue, as you people call that shade of black. There are times I find English confusing. But I speak it well enough to know you call that shade of light black, blue. Both Cheyenne and their Siksika kinsmen you insist on calling Blackfeet think that shade of light black has much medicine. Hear me. I think someone with his moccasin beaded by a careless woman lost these beads to a clump of soap weed as he led his pony up a steep rise. I saw one hoofprint earlier. That is why I was gazing down with the eyes of an eagle to begin with."

Longarm put the spoon down again as he said dryly, "I figured you were straining your eyes some. Was the boy who lost a moccasin stitch leading a shod or unshod pony?"

Laughing Raven took his mementos back to put away as he asked in a disgusted tone, "Why would anyone on the warpath want to ride with his pony shod? It's hard enough to avoid leaving tracks when your pony runs as

Wakan-Tonka intended ponies to run on soft sod. I was told you knew more than most of your kind about such matters."

"Hell, I was a fair tracker as a boy back in West-by-God-Virginia. We used to hunt all sorts of critters, and the old flintlocks we had then only fired once. So you had to know what you were about when you were hunting coon or fox."

Laughing Raven nodded soberly and said, "Both are almost as wise and tricky as Old Man Coyote. What might tracking coon and fox have to do with tracking Contraries?"

Longarm drained the last of his coffee, signaled the Greek for another cup, and explained, "A heap. There was this one old fox every man, boy and redbone hound in the county hunted high and low before a sharp old-timer figured out what that fool fox was up to. You see, we had us a heap of split-rail fences back home. They zigzagged all over creation. That sly old fox had taken to running along the top rails of the fences, leaving no scent on either side for the hounds to follow as he worked his way from one chicken run to another."

The Indian chuckled and said, "Wa, that was a fox who'd talked to Old Man Coyote in his youth. How did you ever catch him if he left no trail for your dogs to follow? Did someone see him as he ran along a fence that way?"

Longarm shook his head and said, "He hunted at night. The old hunter who figured out what he was doing caught him easy once he figured it out. All he had to do, then, was set a spring trap atop a fence rail, near a gap where the old fox had to do some running and jumping. The old fox just ran into her a few nights later. But I don't know about pineapple pie. I'd best stick with the apple pie my innards are more familiar with."

Laughing Raven said, "I hate all kinds of pie. You people would have good teeth, like me, if you liked the taste of fat as much as you liked sugar. Anyway, I don't think those Contraries could be riding along fence rails, out here. There are only a few barbed-wire fences and birds have enough trouble perching on them. Hear me. I have thought about them following the rails of the Iron Horse to avoid leaving tracks. There are no rails leading to any good hiding places. The Americans aboard the Iron Horse would have said something by now if many Indians of any kind were on the road of the Iron Horse. I think you should forget that sly fox you hunted long ago and faraway. They have dry grass, a lot of dry grass, to ride across in every direction. I don't see how we could set a trap for anyone. It will be hard enough to track them down. They are not alone out there. There are cows, many cows. There are even a few antelope and buffalo left. There are other riders, many other riders, all leaving pony tracks all over the place."

Longarm swallowed some more coffee before he said, "That's why I asked if the rider as lost them moccasin beads was leading an unshod pony. The other night I brushed with some for-certain Indians who seemed to be aboard *shod* stock. Your turn."

Laughing Raven ordered more coffee and cranked some flour into it as he said, "Horse thieves. They hadn't had time to take the horseshoes off yet. Even when we are not looking for any trouble, none of us plains nations like to slow our ponies down with useless American iron on their feet. The rider whose trail I cut was riding the good old way. His beads read Cheyenne. That is all I know for certain."

"You don't know *that* much, for *certain*, as soon as

you study on it," Longarm said. "I've seen those jars of beads they have on many a trading post counter. They come in all kinds of colors. The women buy all sorts of colors. The gal as beaded that one set of moccasins you're so excited about could have made 'em mostly white, with Lakota medicine signs trimmed in blue, green, or, hell, lavender for all we really know. Us lawmen ain't supposed to let ourselves be prejudiced, see?"

"No. I don't know the meaning of that last big word."

Longarm explained, "Them cowhands as jumped you out on the lone prairie were prejudiced. They figured that as long as they'd heard there was Indian trouble, and you looked like an Indian, they ought to give you some trouble. It ain't just unfair. It can lead a hunter to the wrong tree. We got to keep it in mind that we ain't after just any old Indian. We got to single out the one sort of Indian that's really acting mean, and where in thunder is that apple pie I ordered?"

The Greek had of course been listening to their conversation all this time. So as he cut a slice of pie for Longarm he asked, with a sardonic look, why Longarm talked so rudely about Sons of Hellas if he was so lacking in prejudice. Longarm smiled thinly and said, "Hell, it don't matter whether anybody teases you, an Irishman, or even a Chinee. None of you have to worry about the army charging in to bust all your crockery in the near future. Prejudice against Indians is more serious. Nobody is funning when they accuse an *Indian* of acting the least bit odd."

Chapter 7

At the livery, Longarm decided to have them saddle the cordovan with Morgan lines for him again. Laughing Raven agreed his own paint could use some more rest and settled on a black mare he insisted on calling blue. The colored hands refused to peel her shoes off for him. Longarm convinced the big Crow it wasn't worth a fight. It wasn't easy. Laughing Raven was still bitching about being stuck with an infernal American plow horse as they mounted up out front.

But before they could ride anywhere, a town youth packing a six-gun and an arm band with "Special Police" written on it joined them afoot to tell Longarm the regular deputy and the city council wanted a word with him before he left town.

So the three of them went over to the town hall. The two federal lawmen tethered their ponies and followed the kid inside.

There, they found a small but worried meeting in progress at a trestle table set up on the platform they used for anything from a serious trial to a presentation by the local high school drama class. Longarm grabbed a folding chair. Laughing Raven sat on the floorboards in one corner to smoke in obvious annoyance at the delay.

Longarm was anxious to be on more serious business as well. So he said so. An old geezer who seemed to be in charge pointed at a younger geezer seated next to the only woman at the table.

The townsman in charge said, "We was hoping the damned old sheriff or at least our town marshal would be back by now. You being the only serious lawman left in these parts, we'd like your educated opinion on a matter afore this board. These folk would be the Princess Olga and her road manager, Mr. Gradey. They want a permit to set up their tent show on the edge of town. Do you reckon we ought to let 'em?"

Longarm turned to the gal. She wasn't bad looking if you liked 'em fairly well padded and staring at you dark and mysterious with big old Gypsy eyes from under a veiled riding derby. He asked her what sort of a show they might be talking about. Her road manager, a mite more beefy and not near as pretty, cut in with, "Her Highness don't talk such good English, pal. What we call Princess Olga's Rooshin Circus is a one-ring show. All acts decent enough for kids to watch. We got no elephants, lions, or other dangerous critters, unless you count trained bears. Rooshin bears, not grizzlies, tame as anything and twice as smart. We got clowns, of course, and a Hungarian as swallows swords and eats fire. The only important act we want to show the good folk here in Sheridan is Princess Olga, herself. She do wear tights, it's true. But I assure you not an inch of her shows below the neckline as she rides around the ring on her white horses, two of 'em at the same time. It would be a crying sin to deprive the kiddies of this town of such an educational experiment!"

A member of the town council chimed in, "We ain't worried about the little lady putting on a dirty show,

106

Gradey. I seen the princess perform in Gillette last summer and she surely rides nice, considering she's standing up most of the time. The only question before this house is the safety of both you show folk and our own kith and kin. We just told you the Cheyenne has risen and Lord only knows where all our lawmen might be right now."

Gradey insisted, "But you say Mr. Long, here, is the law."

So Longarm explained, "Only federal. The princess don't need a permit from me. If we're just talking safety, I got to study on that. Aside from your circus performers, might you have anything in the way of armed security men traveling with you?"

Gradey looked uncertain and decided, "Well, just about all our roustabouts have been picked for muscle and most of 'em have at least a gun to wear in town after the show, if the town is at all tough. I can't say we can afford our own private police force, like the Ringlings and other big outfits, if that's what you had in mind."

Longarm said it was, but asked, "How many armed men can you put in the field, counting tough clowns, should push come to shove?"

Gradey spoke softly to the princess. In French. Longarm could tell her French was better than Gradey's. Longarm knew before Gradey could tell him that the road show had around forty men with it, tough enough to matter.

As Gradey relayed the fighting figures to him Longarm was already thinking ahead of him. He nodded and said, "Nobody has yet reported half that number of Contraries riding in a bunch. Of course, there may well be more than one bunch. But I doubt they'd be hitting hither and yon in separate raiding parties if they felt any call to bunch up."

"Then you reckon it's safe?" asked the one old geezer.

To which Longarm felt obliged to reply simply, "Nope. On the other hand we can't let a few fool Indians grind commerce to a total halt out here. I don't like the notion of a tent show on the edge of town, lit up so musical and tempting. Ain't there, say, a vacant lot, closer in, you could let these folk use?"

The town council agreed, after some argument, there were at least three such safer sites. One an abandoned coal mine with sheds the performers could use as well. So Longarm said, "There you go. If those Contraries were up to hitting a town entire, they'd have doubtless done so by now, with your law riding posse and all. I can't say it's impossible. But I can't see how anyone in the center of town could be much safer at home in bed than all together watching a tent show at a given time. You might want a lookout posted here and there around the edges of town whether there's a show going on or not. Otherwise, I'd say this little lady has as much right to ride two horses at once as anyone else may have to dig coal or drink suds after dark. Can I go, now? Me and old Laughing Raven have to scout for them Indians further out if it's all the same to you."

The town council agreed and the old geezer pounded the table to announce the meeting was over. As everyone but Laughing Raven got up to mill about, Longarm tried to ease on out without stepping on too many toes. Then the princess blocked his way to call him nice things in both Russian and French. He ticked his hat brim and smiled down at her to say, "Aw, mush, ma'am." The last thing he expected a Russian princess to do was throw her arms around him and haul him in for a big wet kiss. But, being a gent of the old school, Longarm thought it only right to kiss her back. So he did. She was padded just about as good as he'd expected, albeit a mite firmer than she looked, in a ruffled black bodice. When she put some tongue into her passion he decided it was time to go hunt Indians, if ever he meant to, this night. She didn't fight to keep him from performing his duty. He'd noticed that time he'd been bodyguarding Miss Sarah Bernhardt and her outfit that gals as spoke French kissed sort of sassy, even out of bed.

Once outside with Laughing Raven, Longarm tried to put all such French notions out of his mind, since he doubted any fool Indian they tracked down would want to kiss him in any fashion. Laughing Raven waited until they'd crossed the Burlington tracks before he asked, morosely, where they might be headed.

Longarm lit the last cheroot he figured he'd be able to smoke safely in the dark, this close to the brighter lights of Sheridan, and said, "The hills to the west, of course. If we can hunker down on some higher ground near Little Wolf's camp on the Tongue, we may just be able to spy someone riding in or out, backwards, aboard shod or unshod ponies. Have you got a better plan?"

The older lawman said, "Yes. Any plan is better than squatting on some hogback like a pair of damned carrion crows!"

Longarm pointed out, "You can't leave much dead meat on the prairie without them crow-birds spotting it from a distance, you know."

But Laughing Raven insisted, "We could watch for many days, many, and not see anything, even if there was something to see. Hear me. If Little Wolf is speaking straight there are no Contraries riding in or out of his camp. If his tongue is forked, he still won't let anybody see them doing so. It only takes a few minutes to put on paint or take it off. If we see any riders coming or going within half a day's ride of that Cheyenne camp, they will look like innocent hunting parties."

Longarm took a thoughtful drag on his smoke before he said, "There's only so many serious deer hunters one might expect to see in a bunch, pard."

"They could ride in and out in small parties. They could join up and put on their paint too far from camp for even a real bird to see. I do not know if even one Contrary is attached to Little Wolf's band. I do know there must be at least two such bands."

Longarm didn't ask how Laughing Raven surmised as much as he already had. Unless they had some trick that put that old fence-running fox back home to shame, there was simply no way one band could hit so far and wide with nobody noticing them between raids. He said, "All right. They hit down by Cedar Creek, got the posse to chase after 'em there, and hit next near Parkman, sixty miles northwest by crow and farther by pony or even railroad. Once the fool posse was on its way to Parkman, they raided that spread as far the other way, over to Campbell County. And leave us not forget the anxious evening some damned pest with a bow and arrow got me and some others, just north of town, at about the same damned time!"

Laughing Raven nodded and said, "Three bands, at least. Maybe two Contrary bands and some Suicide Boys out to count coup when they learned of other bands on the warpath. I think it is time to talk to someone who may know what's going on."

Longarm snorted in disgust and said, "You're a great

help. Of *course* we get to question one or more of the pests, as soon as we can catch one, in shape to talk. But let's eat this apple a bite at a time, damn it. To catch that first one, we have to cut his damned trail, don't we?"

"Maybe not," Laughing Raven replied. "I was on my way to talk to a member of the Contrary Lodge when those cowboys jumped me."

"You mean the sport you were trailing so close with one hoofprint and two glass beads to lead you to him?" asked Longarm.

Laughing Raven said, "Don't be silly. I save Wanted posters, too. The old man I have in mind lives with his daughter and her husband, an American, like you. They had to take him in when he got too old and stiff to live the old way. The girl is good, as all our girls are. Her American husband must be fond of her. Her father is old, dirty, and crazy, crazy. But he may remember some of the raids he rode on with the Contrary Lodge in the Shining Times."

Longarm frowned and asked, "Hold on. Are these Indian pals of yours *Crow*?"

To which Laughing Raven replied, "You call us that. We don't. Of course the girl and her old father are of my own nation. Would you expect me to have Lakota or Cheyenne friends?"

"I reckon that would be asking too much. I just wasn't expecting a Contrary Lodge among you peaceable Crow."

Laughing Raven scowled and said, "Bite your tongue, paleface! Hear me. In the Shining Times nobody was as warlike as my people, nobody! We fought everybody from the Utes, our favorite enemies, to the lying Lakota who said bad things about us. Of *course* we had all the fighting lodges everyone else had. How

111

dare you call us woman-hearted! I thought you Americans were our allies. Hear me! We warriors of the Sparrow Hawk Clan have taken more hair for the Great White father than anybody, anybody! You never would have beaten the Lakota Confederacy without us!"

Longarm replied, soothing, "I doubt many Lakota would argue about that, old son. All I was out to establish is whether this old Crow we're going to visit knows the rules and regulations of the infernal Contrary Lodge. How far a ride are we talking?"

"Not far. Halfway between here and where those cowboys jumped me. I was on my way to visit Bloody Bladder when they caught me with my guard down. I was on federal cattle range, not any damned reserve. I told you the old man was living off the blanket with his daughter and her American husband."

So Longarm let Laughing Raven take the lead and, for a ride an Indian considered short, they rode quite a spell over rolling grass-covered swells and timbered draws as the skinny moon got ever higher without really lighting things up enough to matter.

During a trail break Longarm found out the retired Bloody Bladder was so called because he'd once smacked an enemy war chief in the face with an antelope bladder filled with dog blood. The Crow had thought that funny as hell. The enemy leader had of course been so mortified he sent the Crow some tribute ponies and asked them to make their boys fight fair, next time. Even Longarm could see how embarrassing it might feel to have a ferocious Crow get inside one's guard, raise what looked like a war club for a killing blow, only to have it burst in your face and wash off all your war paint with dog blood. Indians had made warfare a sort of amusing sport in the Shining Times. The point had been to prove how brave you were. Killing folk had just been added spice, like the fact that the bull might really gore the matador in the midst of his fancy cape-work if he didn't show real style.

Dying for another smoke but considering it poor style at a time like this, Longarm pondered Indian ways as he chased the ass of Laughing Raven's pony at an uncomfortable but mile-eating trot. His Crow companion had only been bragging a decimal dot when he'd said his nation had licked the Lakota with just a little help from the U.S. Army. The dumbest thing the Lakota had ever done had been one hell of a break for the white man.

As Longarm understood it, the Lakota, Dakota, or Nakota, as they pronounced it west to east, had once upon a time been a woodland nation living on deer and wild rice along the Great Lakes, further east. Nobody much had lived on the Great Plains before the Comanche lifted some Spanish horses in the 1700s and invented the buffalo-hunting and decidedly wild Indian. Called Sioux by their Chippewa enemies in the lake country, the Lakota had drifted ever westward because of pressure from their red and white enemies, and just as likely because hunting and fishing on ponies in open country had been more fun. There hadn't been any Crow Nation, that early.

Longarm and likely most Indians found the spiritual notions of a folk without any written scriptures sort of confusing. But it seemed the elders who kept the oral traditions had at least a few generally agreed-on notions. Lakota meant "friends" or "allies." As such they were divided into clans, such as turtles, foxes, and in one important case, sparrow hawks or crows, depending on who was translating. It had something to do with the never-to-be-broken incest regulations of Wakan-Tonka, the Great Goodness, Great Spirit, or Big Medicine. Dream singers were allowed to argue about that.

But there was no argument about *incest*. Like most Indians, the Lakota considered it the sin of sins. Folk who thought stealing and killing for sport was okay had to have *something* Wakan-Tonka just could not allow, most likely. Members of the same clan might or might not ride with any band. In peacetime a band of, say, thirty hunters and their dependents ate just about all there was to eat within a day's hunt. All members of a band who belonged to the same clan—the lodges were more like clubs and didn't count—were considered cousins. So turtle boys courted sparrow hawk or fox gals and vice versa. You weren't supposed to even flirt with a gal of your *own* clan.

But human nature being human, it had apparently come to pass that at some big gathering an important Lakota of the sparrow hawk clan had spied a strange gal he really fancied. He played his old nose flute at her until the feeling was mutual. But then, perhaps a mite late, they discovered to their dismay that they were both sparrow hawks or crows. That should have been the end of it, as Lakota saw it. But love will find a way, and even Longarm could see that sweethearts from seperate bands, who'd never met before, could hardly be *close* cousins. So the love-sick, young, and above all powerful chief married up with the pretty gal anyway, and his own kin had no choice but to cast dogshit and curses at him, or back him up.

They backed him up. The young couple rode off with their few friends to form their own band. They might have stayed Lakota if the hard-liners of the main bands had let them. But they never. They told the outcasts they were no longer friends and, worse yet, called them sister-fuckers. So by the time any whites came along to care, the outcast Lakota had grown big enough to become the Crow Nation, never anywhere near the size of the Lakota Nation, but making up for it in the bitter hatred and fighting skills of a picked-on people. They'd taken to scouting for the army as a duck takes to water, with results no dream singer had ever had a vision about when it had been so much fun to jeer at a sort of Indian version of Romeo and Juliet. But the more Longarm studied on it, the more it seemed an old Crow, who was a Lakota or Sioux in all but name, ought to know the secret rites of the same.

But things didn't work out that way. For as they topped a dimly moonlit rise they spied an orange glow beyond the next one and Laughing Raven reined in to say, "Hear me. That is a fire. A big one, big. Grass, and more, must be burning over that way."

Longarm suggested they ride windwards and work around it. But Laughing Raven sighed and said, "We have no reason to. I think it must be the place I was leading you to that burns so bright. Heya, let us go see!"

They did. They circled upwind to approach the cow spread in a draw across blackened sod that had already burnt out. Downwind to the east a line of burning grass outlined the smoldering ruins of the sod house and outbuildings, smoky black. The two lawmen tethered their ponies to the charred post of a barbwire dooryard fence and moved in the rest of the way afoot, their saddle guns at port with rounds in their chambers.

It was a wipeout. Here and there flames still flickered inside the roofless shell of the main soddy. But most of the roof and interior had been reduced to glowing embers. A sewing machine in one corner still glowed red-hot. Some longer lengths of still-burning wood figured to be roof beams or bed rails. Three lumps of twisted charcoal seemed to be stinking more than they were still smouldering. Laughing Raven said quietly, "I think that smaller one near the red-hot shotgun barrel must have been the girl I told you about. All three went down with guns in their hands. All three died well, at least. I can't tell which of the two bigger bodies was red or white, can you?"

Longarm swallowed and said, "Not hardly. But you're right. All three went down fighting." Then he wet the tips of his fingers and tried to pry the arrow point he'd just noticed from the doorjamb next to him. It was too hot.

Laughing Raven said, "Leave it. I see it. There is another one, here at my feet. It must have been stuck in the door, before the door burned away. They are both trading post points. There must be more stuck in the three bodies. Do you think the numbers are important?"

Longarm shook his head and said, "Where they come from might be. Do you reckon the Cheyenne still living wild along the Tongue get in to trade for arrowheads a lot?"

Laughing Raven shrugged and said, "Little Wolf's band has nothing to trade. There are no buffalo robes to be gathered near here. Nobody wants beaver pelts anymore. The price they could get on fox skins and deer hides would not be worth the risk of leaving their last stronghold."

"You mean that leaves Little Wolf's band out?" asked Longarm thoughtfully.

"No. One parfleche can hold many arrowheads, many. One or more of Little Wolf's young men could have bought or stolen plenty of them when they were all down at Fort Reno. Steel broadheads are meant for serious targets, like buffalo or people. You hunt deer and even weaker game with wood or rabbit-bone tips. No tips at all for birds. I think someone meant these steel broadheads for killing people. I don't know if they came from Little Wolf's camp or not. I do think this was the work of Contrary riders, though. There was no good reason, none, to kill these people."

Longarm objected. "Two of 'em were Crow. Ain't the Cheyenne on the outs with all Crow?"

Laughing Raven looked disgusted and said, "You try hard to understand us. But hear me, you do not understand us. The girl was not a Crow anymore. She had married an American, in the Jesus Lodge. A woman belongs to the nation of her husband. So she was American, to us. The Cheyenne are not at war with America this fall. Old Bloody Bladder had not fought for many summers. He was living your way, with his American daughter. How could anyone count coup on such a person? The women would laugh at him if he danced with the scalp of a harmless old cripple. That is how I know Contraries did this. They do everything, everything the *wrong way.*"

Longarm stepped clear of the ruins, shot a glance at the empty corral, and said, "Well, whoever they were, they ran off all the stock. The county law can figure out who might own any range cows left, out yonder in the dark. How do you feel, now, about staking out that Cheyenne camp to the west?"

Laughing Raven said flatly, "You go, if you want. I do not play games with Cheyenne. I am riding back to Sheridan to wait for the army. When they come I will offer to scout Little Wolf for them. It won't matter, then, if he knows anything about what happened here or not. Wa, I *like* to kill Cheyenne, don't you?"

Longarm replied, "Oh, some of 'em are all right. It hardly seems fair to pepper anyone with Hotchkiss guns before you know whether they're innocent or guilty, and Little Wolf did say none of his young men were riding contrary."

Laughing Raven headed back for thier ponies with Longarm in bemused tow as he proclaimed, "Hear me. All Cheyenne deserve to die. All Cheyenne are fork-tongued. Cheyenne *means* 'Those Who Talk Funny,' in my own language."

Longarm protested, "Sure, but that's only on account they enlisted in the Lakota Confederacy talking a different lingo. A man can talk Spanish or even French without being a liar, can't he?"

The big Crow said, "I don't know. All I know is that Cheyenne talk and act different from anyone on my side. Heya, let's go see if the blue sleeves will let us help them when they wipe out Little Wolf, once and for all!"

So Longarm rode back to Sheridan with him, if only to see if he could work things out a less disgusting way.

Chapter 8

They got there in the wee small hours. But although the first cock had yet to crow, there was a heap of hustle and bustle going on along a railroad siding as the two night riders crossed the tracks. Laughing Raven said he was sleepy and rode on to his bunk at the lockup. Longarm was commencing to feel a mite saddle sore, and he'd been considering how much fun it might be to wake little Norma up for some early ham and eggs or anything else she might have to offer. But as he saw all those freight cars being emptied by torchlight he just had to go see why. So he dismounted and tethered to a crossing sign to amble over afoot, lighting the first smoke he'd been able to enjoy for most of a night.

As he drifted into the crowd around the freight cars, he saw that as he'd suspected it was the tent show of Princess Olga. He didn't see her amid the confusion. It seemed only natural that they had to unload their circus train at trackside, on this edge of town. He wasn't half as sure they ought to be pitching their big old tent just fifty-odd yards from the tracks, even if it was in the middle of a vacant lot. He drifted over to some roustabouts driving a tent stake to ask them who'd told 'em to set up here instead of the safer lot near the center of the settlement. They answered him in some odd lingo. So he moved on.

Some smaller tents had already been pitched on the far side of the main one. He stepped around a cage full of sleepy bears and spied the princess and her road manager, Gradey, talking in the lamp-lit fly of one dinkier tent. She looked tired and somehow prettier as she stood there in a work smock instead of all decked out in frills to impress the townsfolk. She spotted him first and waved him over with a French yoo-hoo. As he joined them, Gradey turned with a more thoughtful smile to ask how come he was up so early, adding, "The show won't be ready to open this side of noon. You won't need a ticket, of course."

Longarm said, "I didn't get up special to pester you folk. I was off scouting Indians. Bad ones. We just found a cow spread burnt-out with three dead bodies in it. How come you're setting up here, with nothing between you and a heap of rolling prairie but some railroad tracks? Wasn't it agreed both you and your customers would be safer in more civilized parts of Sheridan?"

He could see the princess was trying to follow the conversation without much luck as Gradey explained, "Don't blame me if some kid eating a candy apple busts a tooth on an arrowhead. It seems the old fogey who owns that vacant mining property we were talking about thinks he has a *real* gold mine. He asked us more for the use of his land than we figure to make selling tickets. The same goes for other lots closer to the hub of the universe. One of the council members said we could use this land free. So here we are. I don't like it any better than you do, but we have to set up *some* damned where."

He translated some of that for the princess. She smiled up at Longarm and tried for, "Oui, ze show must go on, non?"

Longarm smiled back, it was hard not to, and said, "I've been told that, more than once, by show folk. What I've never figured was *why* the show must go on. Common sense says some things have to be at least as important."

She just looked blank. Gradey explained, "She don't savvy a word of English." Then he said, "I'd sure like to stay here and translate. But we were talking about a heap of chores I had to tend to when you joined us. So I'd best get cracking. Would you like to tag along, Deputy?"

Longarm said he'd watched them pitch lots of tents when he'd been in the army. So Gradey shrugged and wandered off with his clipboard to yell orders at everyone. Longarm and Princess Olga stared awkwardly at one another for a time. Then she tried some German on him, and when that didn't work, surprised him pleasantly by asking, *"Habla Usted español?"*

He replied in border Mex, "My Spanish is much better than my French, Princesa. Where might a Russian lady have learned such fine Spanish?"

She dimpled up at him in the soft light to answer, "In Spain, of course. Before I was left this little show by my poor late father we toured all the capitals of Europe and, to tell the truth, many small villages where the people had little to spare for amusements. I thought business would be better in this vast country of yours. So I have been touring it for a little over a year, now."

He asked how business had been. She sighed and said, "Very good, as far as ticket sales go. Even your working classes are rich, over here. But the travel expenses were something I had not considered. In truth I have barely been able to break even with all this moving about. In Europe we are used to performing in one place, longer. Over here, we are most fortunate to stay more than a day or so, in one of your larger towns."

He glanced away from her, toward the tracks, and asked if she owned her own train. She said she did but that the railroad still charged a heap to haul her and her private cars all over creation. She said, "It costs less to get around, further east. But we are more of a novelty and sell more tickets out here in your western provinces. They look so small, on the map, and take so much time and money to move around in. We never spent a whole day moving from one showplace to another back in France."

He nodded knowingly and said, "Things do come sort of far apart out here on the High Plains. I thought you were Russian, Princesa. You sound as if you spent more time in west Europe with your Russian bears and horses."

She answered demurely, "Es verdad. Mostly France and Spain, where both I and my beasts are more of a novelty. Would you keep it a secret if I told you I am not really a Russian princess?"

He grinned down at her and said he was just swell at keeping secrets for the unfair sex. So she confided, "I am really part Georgian and part Tatar. In Georgia anyone who owns more than one horse is a prince. My late father was the black sheep of a prosperous Georgian— how do you say it?—ranchero?"

Longarm started to ask a dumb question. Then he recalled there was a Georgia in Russia, too, and told her, "Your tale sounds fair to me. A lot of men I've met from our own Georgia have told me they used to be colonels, and I've never met one who wasn't at least a captain. So I won't tell anyone you're not related to the czar. How many guards do you have posted on the other side of the tracks, Princesa?"

She looked blank and said she didn't understand. He asked her whether her American road manager had even mentioned Indians and she said, "Si, we were just talking about that. Señor Gradey said there had been some Indian raids up this way as well and asked if I did not think it wise to forget holding our show here, since we can't get a site less exposed to the open plain. I told him we have no choice. The show must go on. Not because I am a woman of tradition, but because I am a woman who likes to pay her crew. In truth I need the money and there seems to be Indian trouble or at least rumors of Indian trouble all up and down the railroad line this fall. So far, we have yet to even see a tame Indian, and whether the rumors are true or not, we still have to eat. Do you think me a silly woman, Señor?"

He said, "My friends call me Custis, and I was wondering why the show had to go on. I'll talk to Gradey and the town law about posting some gun hands further out in the grass, Princesa. I can see you're busy. So mucho gusto with your show this afternoon, and I'm sort of looking forward to watching you ride two horses at once, in tights."

She batted her lashes at him and said, "Gracias. When a woman never expects to see thirty again, such forward remarks can do wonders for her ego. I do look well in tights. I have been considering ending my riding act with my own version of Mazeppa. Only the riding part, of course. You know of that legend?"

He smiled uncertainly and told her, "Just that last part about Mazeppa riding off, naked, tied to a wild

123

stallion upside down. It seems every actress with a decent figure and no fear of horses has been playing Mazeppa, lately. Correct me if I'm wrong, but in the original story, wasn't Mazeppa a *man* from Poland, who they treated so unfriendly?"

She twinkled her big dark eyes at him and said, "You *are* well-read, for a Yanqui. I think it was Sarah Bernhardt who first decided it would add some spice to the drama if they bound a seemingly nude woman instead of a man to the wild stallion."

He laughed and said, "I can see why. I've seen Miss Sarah in tights that weren't even flesh colored. But are you sure Sheridan is ready for such excitement, Princesa? I know that you'd really be in control of the horse and not really tied helpless. But should you gallop even a short ways out on the prairie in such a tempting condition . . . I don't think you'd better do it."

She assured him she hadn't made her mind up, yet. So he told her not to and then, since she held her hand out expectantly, he kissed the back of it and headed back to his pony.

He rode the cordovan to the livery and made sure they rubbed it down good while they watered and oated it. By this time cocks were commencing to bitch all over town about the coming dawn, and he was looking forward to a few winks in little Norma's bed. He wanted some of Norma, while he was at it. A night in the saddle had that effect on a man's privates, if he was young and healthy.

But first he stopped at the all-night Western Union office to see if they had any less certain forecasts for him. They did. Having been up all night the red-eyed clerks on duty were a font of information, wired or just gossiped in.

The big posse had finally made it back, around midnight, and so while the sheriff and town marshal were no doubt planning on sleeping late, it was good to know there'd be a serious number of lawmen about should Princess Olga decide to tear out of her show tent in tights. The news about the army was more bothersome. The troops figured to show up in Sheridan late in the afternoon. If he couldn't get them to attend the evening show, Longarm knew they'd go charging into Little Wolf's camp before he could prove anything one way or the other.

There was nothing he could do about it, this early. He had no instructions from Billy Vail, since his Denver office didn't have good reason to think he was still in Sheridan, let alone the back of a gun shop. So he headed for the gun shop before anyone might notice.

But someone did. Another fool kid with an arm band caught up with Longarm halfway to Norma's to tell him Miss Mira, the blonde assistant coroner, had heard he was back in town and wanted a word with him, pronto. He asked the kid if she was waiting for him at the morgue. He was mildly surprised to learn she wanted him at her living quarters, instead. There was nothing to do but stride over to her house and see what she wanted.

The messenger she'd sent peeled off along the way. So he was alone and thus safe to say, as she greeted him in her doorway, "I thought you said you never wanted to see me again, ma'am."

She was wearing a dressing gown, loosely tied, and her long blonde hair was down. But she said, "This is business. Come in." So he went.

Inside, she sat him on a leather chesterfield near the fireplace. Neither the fire nor any lamps were lit. But they could see one another well enough in the dawn

125

light through her lace curtains. She sat down beside him and poured coffee for them both as she said, "I heard you and that Indian were out scouting last night. The posse rode in around midnight with another body. From his clothing and where they said they'd found him, near the railroad tracks, I'd say he was a hobo who made a terrible mistake by dropping off too far from town. He'd been scalped, of course. I couldn't find either arrow or bullet wounds when I performed the autopsy. Your turn."

Longarm sipped some coffee gratefully before he said, "Easy. One man, alone and unarmed in the middle of nowhere hardly would have called for arrowing or gunning. Say they just hit him over the head with the proverbial blunt instrument and then scalped the same spot. What would you have left?"

She grimaced and said, "I'll buy that. I'm just not up to sawing open his skull, and it's an established fact that he was dead when they found him. I can't see another hobo lifting his scalp, can you?"

He shrugged and said, "Indians seem to do that more often, ma'am. Was his hair lifted Lakota or Cheyenne style?"

She wrinkled her nose and asked, "Good heavens, is there a difference?"

To which he replied with a sober nod, "There sure is. Lakota scalp neater. They just take a patch a little bigger than a silver dollar. Cheyenne take about all the hair there is. They mutilate at least the right hand as well. You got a better look at the poor cuss than I did."

She nodded and said, "His hands were just dirty. Now that you mention it, he was scalped sort of in between. I'd hardly call the results neat, but they tore off a sort of triangular patch the size of, oh, say a folded kerchief."

He said, "A coming train must have spooked 'em, then. Or maybe Contraries scalp crazy as well. I hope you ain't too tired, ma'am. I have three more bodies for you, now that the town law has some manpower. You know a white man raising beef a few hours to the northwest, with an Indian wife and father-in-law?"

"I know of them. I think their name is Watkins."

"Was," he said. "Past tense. From the way the fire had worked downwind by the time we found 'em, I'd say they were hit well before midnight. If it was the same band as hit that hobo they sure had a busy night, didn't they?"

She grimaced and said, "They did indeed! My God, I thought at least a squaw-man would be safe from Indians around here!"

"Watkins must have thought that, too. An Indian just told me real warriors thought it sort of cheap to count coup on women and cripples. Of course, everyone kills innocent bystanders, and they might have been after the white man in particular. You see, all the chiefs have said they're at peace with us right now. So it's sort of *contrary* to kill whites."

He inhaled some more coffee before he mused, half to himself, "Easier, too. I wonder if, once they get a good Indian war going, those Contrary riders will feel obliged to stay out of it."

"The army should be here by nightfall, Custis. Why not let *them* worry about it?"

He scowled and said, "They never worry all that much. Little Wolf ain't got the manpower to stand off half a troop, and they're sending in a full battalion of cav with a battery of field guns. It's tough to win medals and promotions in a peacetime army. So them poor Cheyenne are fixing to get shot to glory whether they want a fight or not!"

She sighed and said, "Well, they are off any reservation, and *some* Indians around here have certainly been spoiling for a fight with us."

He shook his head and said, "It's the yellow legs, not any *us* that'll gain the dubious glory along the Tongue, ma'am. I fear old Little Wolf has been set up for honors he might not deserve. He's a mean old cuss. He told me his fool self he didn't like us at all. But fair is fair and that band has never attacked nobody since they holed up along the Tongue a few summers ago."

She insisted, "You mean *openly*, don't you? I'd hardly say that poor hobo they brought in had been attacked by *peaceful* Indians. Maybe the old sneak is just afraid to declare open war on us. So he's been sending out those sneaky raiding parties, wearing Contrary paint. Is there any law that says a chief who hates us can't act sneaky?"

Longarm nodded and said, "Yep. Indian law ain't written on stone, or even paper. But it's just as binding. Riding with an Indian lawman has made me think a heap on Indian notions of right and wrong. Little Wolf is more an old-time Indian than my pal, Laughing Raven, and even Laughing Raven thinks all this Contrary stuff is just disgusting and, worse yet, yellow-bellied. Little Wolf is a Crooked Lance. Custom requires them to fight as gallant as our own ancient knights. As I study back on the little anyone knows about the Contrary Lodge, *they* were supposed to act brave or even braver in the Shining Times. Us whites never got to learn much about the Contrary Lodge. They were usually the first ones down in a serious fight. Riding backwards and swatting at enemies with silly weapons worked better against other Indians than it ever did the U.S. Army or even a tough cowhand. When you smack a white man across the face with a feather duster or even a blood-filled bladder, he's more inclined to kill you than feel you've made a fool of him."

"You've lost me, Custis. Are these Contraries of yours supposed to be devil worshippers or *clowns*, for heaven's sake? None of the victims I've seen, so far, look like they died of mortification. I wasn't around in the Golden Age of the Plains Indian, thank God, but it's my professional opinion that these so-called Contraries we have to worry about, now, are really out for *blood*, not practical jokes!"

She sipped her own cup, brightened, and asked, "Have you considered they might not really *be* members of any mystic lodge, Custis? What if they're just troublemakers?"

He said soberly, "They sure have made enough trouble, for both sides. I already considered that. I can't get it to work. Little Wolf's Indian enemies wouldn't play games with him if they were sore enough to go after him. He's off the reserve with no agent to speak up for him. He'd be fair game for any officially friendly Indian who wanted to take him out. On paper he's a pure renegade. There's an open season on renegade bands. Any Crow or even reservation Lakota who had it in for Little Wolf could just go after him, and count coup on him while they were at it. Getting to count coup on a dead enemy is even more fun than killing him."

She suggested, "What about political enemies, within his band, then?"

So Longarm had to shake his head and explain, "Not hardly. Two good reasons. To begin with, the position of chief ain't all that solid. Half the trouble we've had with Indian treaties derives from the mistaken notion that a chief is something like a king or even a president. Most Indians carry democracy past all common sense. Nobody but maybe an unwed woman or a child has to do a thing the chief says, if they don't really want to. Old Little Wolf rules by common consent, because the others admire him. Any Cheyenne who had command of at least two raiding parties of say a dozen each wouldn't *have* to back-stab Little Wolf out of office. He'd just ask for a vote. There can't be more than thirty or forty braves, all told, in the band, see?"

She nodded and said, "Of Course. I can add up the figures. You said there were two reasons, though."

"Oh," he said, "the second one is easier. Why in thunder would any political rival want the army coming at all of 'em at once? Anyone with a lick of sense could see that stirring up Indian trouble was sure to get the only band of Indians in these parts in trouble. It's mighty hard to be the chief of an extinct band, no matter how much you might want the job, ma'am."

She sighed, put her cup aside to lean back, and told him, "You've convinced me. With no sensible motive, the leaders behind this nonsense have to be just, well, *contrary.* And why have you been calling me ma'am, Custis? I should think that in view of, ah, things that happened earlier, you might address me in more familiar terms."

He stared at her innocently and asked, "Did something all that familiar happen, ma'am? I thought you said it never."

She smiled up at him sensuously to say, "I was hoping I could count on your discretion. I must confess I never expected you to be *that* discreet, lover-man!"

130

He shrugged and said, "I'm about as discreet as anyone I can't arrest ever asks me to be, ah, Mira. But to tell the truth, it'd be a heap easier if nobody changed the rules once the cards had been dealt. As I recall, you told me right in yonder doorway that I was never to darken it again."

She sighed and said, "I was confused and maybe a little frightened after such an unexpected adventure, dear. Haven't you ever had second thoughts after you'd had time to cool off and think back on some reckless delights?"

"Sure," he said, "I'm just as dumb as most men. But I wish you'd make up your mind, one way or the other."

"I have. I really wanted to end it, while we still could, before anyone found out. But then nobody did. I saw you really didn't kiss and tell and, to tell the truth, I wound up acting shameful with my own lonely fingers last night, and it was't at all the same. Don't you suppose, if we were ever so careful about the neighbors, we could maybe, you know, just once in a while?"

He knew better. He'd often cussed himself in the past for not quitting while he was ahead. But being human, and since her gown had already fallen open, and since no woman would ever forgive a man for leaving her in such an undignified position in any case, he just shucked everything he had on from the boots up and rolled his hips between her yawning thighs.

But, of course, he'd no sooner gotten to admiring the contrast between blonde and auburn hair, parted by daylight, before she commenced to moan and groan about how awful it would be if anyone ever found out. He knew she'd come. So he repaid her the compliment, kissed her in a sort of brotherly way, and rolled off to figure out where he might have skimmed that fool Stetson. She sighed and said, "I'm sorry, darling. When I'm feeling passionate I don't care if the whole world wants to watch. But as soon as I feel cool enough to think straight . . ."

He said he understood. He wasn't sure he did. And even though she'd decided, by the time he had his fool coat on again, that maybe just once more wouldn't hurt, he told her they had to be firm and left before the neighbors could run them both out of town on a rail. He didn't see why she had to throw that coffee cup against the door as he shut it after him.

He considered the hotel as he walked back to the center of town. But when he got to the main street he saw Norma's gun shop was open for business and, worse yet, she was standing in her doorway. So he walked on over to give her the business, or, failing that, catch a few hours' sleep before the fool army showed up.

Norma looked mighty pleased to see him. She asked, "Where have you been all this time, darling? You look as if you just had a hard night!"

He smiled sheepishly down at her and said, "The morning was sort of rough, too. I spent most of the time chasing Indians. I may get to chase some more, any time now. Meanwhile, I surely could use a bite to eat, another warm bath, and your lavender-stunk bedsheets, in that order."

It seemed no sooner said than done. Norma hauled him in, fed him sausage and eggs just to prove all women were full of sweet surprises, and the next thing he knew she had him in her bedroom, saying, "You can bathe, later. I'm just gushing for you and I fixed the sign out front to read I'll be open again soon!"

She was open, for him, even sooner. As he got out of

his duds again she said she didn't dare strip herself total, lest some customer wonder why she didn't answer her doorbell soon enough to avoid suspicion. He told her he could be a sport if he wanted to wait until lunchtime. But she just hoisted her skirts, with nothing under them but her black stockings, and to his considerable relief, just the sight of her different-looking love patch inspired him to rise to the occasion. And he was sure glad, by the time they'd finished, that old Mira hadn't gotten more.

Chapter 9

Two-timing could be fun. But acting two-faced felt sort of shitty. So Longarm decided not to invite either gal to see the tent show with him. Disinviting Mira was no problem. But when pretty little Norma woke him at noon with a sweet kiss, coffee, and marmalade on toast, he had to tell her before she could ask that he expected to be too busy that evening, when she closed her shop for the day, to go look at clowns, trained bears and such. Norma sighed sort of wistfully and asked if he minded if she went unescorted after dark. He said he didn't and she was so pleased about him being a good sport that she shucked off her dress and got back between the covers with him, mighty sporty.

As he left her shop a bath and an hour later, he could hear the steam calliope of the tent show playing off in the distance. He couldn't tell if the show had started or whether they were just gathering in the sheaves. He'd seen tent shows before. So while the sound was as tempting as the clang and clatter of a fire engine to the boy still left in him, Longarm trudged on to the county courthouse.

He found the Hall of Records, which was really more like a one-window storeroom on the top floor, and told the teenaged fat gal in charge who he was and that he'd just like to browse if it was all the same to her. She told him he could poke about her file cabinets and, heck, cardboard boxes as much as he liked, as long as he put everything back in the same order he'd found 'em.

As he thanked her and moved around the packing crate she was using as a desk near the door, the kid clerk warned him some of the papers were mighty dusty and asked, sad-eyed, why anyone on earth would want to paw through dusty old files while a circus was in town, if he didn't have to.

He told her, "I have to. I was supposed to come on duty hours ago. But better late than never. I don't know how long I'll be up here, since I ain't sure what I might find. But if you'd like to run over and catch what's left of the show, I'd be proud to hold the fort for you here until you get back."

She smiled, prettier than a fat gal usually managed, and said, "That's ever so gallant of you, sir. But I dasn't. We usually keep this room locked. But of late it's been so busy that they hired me at four dollars a week to keep the files open to public view from noon to suppertime."

He said, "In that case I feel better about some marmalade I just ate. How come things have gotten so busy of late?"

She explained that since it was an election year both parties were inclined to ponder death certificates, land deeds and so on. She said, as if confiding a secret to another teenager, "You have no idea how sneaky some folk can get when it comes to registering to vote. You're not allowed to vote on county matters if you're dead or never lived in the county, but—"

He cut in politely as he could to assure her he knew about such matters, and moved back to see if he could decide where to search first amid the spider webs and paper dust. It might have helped to open that one grimy window. But a lot of papers were piled loose atop boxes and the winds could get tricky across rolling prairie or bare foothills, as one could call Sheridan County one way or the other.

As he opened a drawer of dusty title deeds the bored fat gal drifted back to ask just what he was looking for and if he could use any help. He started to say no. But then he remembered pulling interior guard when he'd have rather gone to town, and told her, "There's a cow spread, or there was, run by a white man who answered to Watkins, ten or fifteen miles out to the northwest. I've been sort of wondering whether he held proper title, to what, or if him and his Indian in-laws were just squatting. Wyoming is still mostly unincorporated territory. So it could work either way."

She turned from him to say, "That'd be under W, in Title-Search, if we have it. Where you put the place puts it in this incorporated county, but, like you just said, there are sure a mess of squatters. He could have even held lawful title, under the Federal Homestead Act, and we still might not have it if he wasn't a voting man."

It would have been insulting to tell the poor little butterball she was smarter than she looked. So Longarm just said, "Good thinking. To vote on county matters, old Watkins would've naturally had to prove his residency by a copy of any federal papers he might have. How do you folk work it if a county resident doesn't own any real estate?"

She hunkered down on her fat rump to slide open a drawer as she explained, "Rent receipts, library cards, kid enrolled in a Sheridan school and such. Most cowhands and all the coal-mine hands can show they're on the payroll of a Sheridan freeholder. Nobody lets us girls vote, anyhow, the mean things."

He assured her they were talking about that, back East, at least, and began to idly thumb through some city deeds just to see if any names matched up with Wanted posters as he asked if they used cross-index, here.

She said she didn't follow his drift. So he explained, "Many a time, something you might want as starts with an A starts with a B, instead. Say you know the address of a property but not the name of the owner. Cross-index files are halfway duplicates as read both ways. A list of names for addresses, a list of lot numbers for names, and so on."

She said it sounded complicated and that they didn't file so fancy in Sheridan County. She added, "I can't find anyone called Watkins listed as a county land owner, Deputy Long."

So he said, "You might try county wedding certificates. Or, better yet, you might try just sitting down some more. There's no need for us both getting dusty, and he might have fibbed about wedding that Crow gal lawfully. Do you have a county plat chart anywhere back here, miss?"

She rose, said her name was Dora, and inched past him into a corner to haul out some maps rolled in pasteboard tubes as she assured him, "I don't mind this at all. It's ever so much more interesting than just sitting. Sometimes I go a whole day up here and nobody comes at all. You'll find the township plats here a heap more complete than further out. The sheriff takes hardly any interest in outlying spreads unless someone's missing stock or beating his wife enough to be heard by distant neighbors."

Longarm chuckled and hauled out a chart to unroll it atop some side-by-side cabinets. Then he brightened and said, "I should have drunk that last cup of black coffee I was offered, Miss Dora. If Watkins was raising cows, he should have been *branding* 'em! Don't you have a register of local brands, under the names of their owners?"

She said she knew the sheriff did and that the county ought to. So as Longarm idly scanned the township plats to see that Norma sure enough owned the lot her shop was set on, the fat gal rooted about in another corner until she suddenly oinked with delight and announced, "I found it! W Bar W, registered to one Wallace Watkins and wife. He only gives his address as the W Bar W spread, though."

Longarm told her she was mighty sharp and added, "I'd say he was just raising beef informal, then. Most men who hold clear title to land like the world to know about it. Lots of old boys start up that way. They have all they own tied up in their herd. Why pay taxes and grazing fees on land as unsettled as most of Wyoming still is?"

She asked, "Why do you suppose he never registered to vote?"

To which Longarm replied, "I just told you. Why pay taxes? It sort of evens out when one considers how many tombstones both parties will vote, next month."

She asked if he wanted her to go through recent wedding permits issued by the county clerk. He shook his head and said, "We don't know how recent Watkins might have married up with a Crow gal, if he ever really did. I can't see a man who doesn't worry about land

138

titles or even voting going through the awkwardness of facing a county clerk with a blushing Indian bride-to-be."

Her eyes got big and her mouth made a bitty rosebud as she asked, "Do you think they could have been living in sin?"

He shrugged and said, "It hardly matters. Watkins, his woman, and his father-in-law would all fit in one kid's casket right now. Likely in Potter's Field, once Miss Mira Hecht gets through looking 'em over. There's no land title to dispute, even if they had any kin who cared. Some other outfit is sure to take in their orphan cows. If it was a big enough herd for that to be a motive, they wouldn't have been such a bitty outfit."

She frowned up at him to say, "I heard this morning that they were wiped out by Indians. Since when do Indians need a *motive* to hurt white folk?"

"Only one of 'em was white, and nobody goes to that much trouble without no reason at all. It's the reasoning of the leader of that bunch, at least, I'm trying to get a handle on. As far as I can see, thanks to you, poor old Watkins wasn't bothering nobody, and all he owned worth stealing was a mess of scrub cows, running loose for anyone to drive off with a lot less trouble. All three of the doubtless terrified folk out there went down with guns in their hands. I doubt they hit anybody. But it was still a chance the raiders didn't have to take. The ones as hit the Rocking Seven the other night were trying to raid stock *without* getting shot at. So how come the W Bar W got hit so much harder? It don't make sense."

The fat girl lowered her lashes and blushed just a mite as she said, "Well, there was that Indian *girl,* and you know how some men treat us poor things when they get the chance."

139

He looked away and said, "Indians have been known to abuse women that way. They're human. But they seldom set out to count coup with that in mind. In any case, they never got the chance to trifle with her that way. One can only hope they shot her before the flames got to her. So it reads like they just rode down on that isolated soddy and treated everyone so mean just for the sake of being mean. There's no sensible reason to burn a gal to cinders no matter what she might have looked like in life."

He was suddenly aware of the cheap perfume the fat gal had on as she told him shyly, "I'd just hate to be burned up by a man who fancied me. Miss Virginia Woodhull writes that a man who'd like to get fresh with a gal should just up and tell her what he wants. Have you ever read anything by Miss Virginia Woodhull?"

He had. He said so, lest the silly little critter offer him a lecture on free love and other such notions. Old Virginia had a lot to answer for, putting her outrageous notions on paper to turn the heads of sweet little things nobody wanted in the first place. Longarm had noticed hardly any really good-looking gals seemed to go along with the notorious Miss Woodhull about gals putting out and paying their own way to show they were smart enough to vote.

He was saved from having to retreat from the fat teenager more than a step or two when a crusty old fart with an Abe Lincoln beard busted in to demand, "I want to see the platted boundary lines of my own derned lot, dang it! I'll show them fool furriners who they're trying to cheat!"

The fat girl looked more scared of the old fart than Longarm saw any reason to be. She gulped and pointed at the chart he'd been scanning atop the cabinets, saying, "It's right here, Mr. Slade. This gent, Deputy Long, was just going over our city lots."

Slade shot Longarm a suspicious look and asked how come. Longarm moved out of his way, saying, "I'm paid to be nosy. It's all yours, pard. Do you mind my asking why you seem to have so much fire under your boiler?"

Slade snapped, "If you'd be the law you may be just the man I'm looking for. Them furriners putting on that tent show near the tracks may be trespassing on my land without my permit!"

Longarm replied, "Do tell? This morning I was told they'd been offered the use of that vacant lot for free. You say you own it and nobody ever asked you?"

Slade snorted in disgust and said, "The lot they're *supposed* to be on belongs to Marcus Dean. The derned fool's on the city council and aims to be a big shot with elections coming on. But I'm in real estate for the *money*. So let me see, here. . . . Oh, I knowed it! You see this line, here? Well, that's the line as divides Dean's lot from mine, and just as I suspected, they got a wagon and some boxes on my side of her!"

Longarm peered over the older man's shoulder to see what all the fuss was about before he decided, "As I read maps, sir, it seems from here that if the main tent is set up in the middle of your neighbor's lot, the show folk must have just put some stuff down, loose, a yard or more further from the tracks than they might have if your own precious soil was fenced and posted."

Slade said, "I don't care if they knowed what they was doing or not. The important thing is that they *done* it. I want you to come with me, now. They're going to have to give me satisfaction or, by gum, I'll have 'em all in jail!"

Longarm had to laugh. So he did. Then he said, more politely, "I fear I'm packing the wrong badge for what you have in mind, Mr. Slade. Parking a wagon in the wrong place ain't a federal offense, as a rule. I hope you understand that as soon as you tell someone about it they'll doubtless be proud to move their gear the few short feet involved."

Slade shook his head and said, "Too late. They've had that wagon and them boxes on my land all morning and they owe me *money*, dang it!"

Longarm sighed and said, "No offense, sir, but you're just spinning your wheels on a greasy track. You can't ask rent from folk you never struck a rent deal with. I'll allow trespassing is against the law, provided and only provided you can prove in court that it was for spite or damaging. I've seen the vacant lots down yonder. There's no fence. There's no sign posted as reads 'Keep Off My Weeds.' There can't be a judge who can read without moving his lips as wouldn't throw your case out of court. Why don't you just tell 'em to move their stuff, polite, and see if they'll offer you a free pass to the show for you and your family?"

Slade stamped a foot, said he didn't *have* a family, and that he'd just go see what the town marshal had to say about all this.

As he stormed out, Longarm chuckled and said, "Oh, well, it was about time the town law got up, anyways. Them posse riders must have rested up by now."

The fat girl said, "Gee, you're brave. Everyone in town is scared of old Sam Slade. He's been known to sue a mother for letting her baby cry too loud."

Longarm shrugged and said, "I know his type. Sheridan has a lot of catching up to do. In Denver we have a place set up to deal with gents like him. They call it the

County Lunatic Asylum. But I reckon he's harmless enough."

She shook her head and said, "Anyone can see you're a stranger in these parts, Deputy Long. You're no doubt right about him being crazy. But he's rich as well as crazy and that makes folk fear him like the old devil he is. They say, even if they can't prove it, that more than one man who crossed him in the past ain't with us no more. You can hire a lot of guns for money and that old man sure has a heap of money!"

Chapter 10

Longarm left the fat girl as pure and bored as he'd found her and headed next for the tent show to see if he could head off some mighty dumb trouble for a prettier lady. But he had to pass the Western Union to get there and he needed some answers to some questions at least as much as Princess Olga needed his services as a pedestrian Paul Revere. So he ducked inside to send some questioning wires. He wasn't sure just what he needed to know from Land Management, but a two-thirds Indian family squatting on federal land they could have filed on, free, had started to skitter about in the back of his mind like one of those fuzz balls you see out of the corner of one eye when common sense tells you nothing ought to be there.

The notion of a likely illiterate squaw-man just gathering a herd in a draw and to hell with taxes or other formalities worked all right when you stared right at it in the light. So Longarm knew the setup had reminded him of something more sinister, or that maybe he was trying to put two or more half-forgotten details from other cases together to form a new pattern. A man's brain tended to do that when he was a born hunter with an ever-active imagination and read more library books than he wanted his pals to know about.

Longarm made sure he wired someone he was on good terms with at Land Management. Even questions from a peace officer tended to just get kicked from pillar to post once some underpaid civil servant at the Interior Department opened 'em in the doorway.

Aware he had to wire with his own money, since his office was already going to give him hell for unauthorized marmalade and such when he was supposed to be in Denver by now, Longarm tried to cover as many angles regarding federal homestead claims in these parts as he could, in as few words as possible. He could only hope his pal at Land Management would understand the message was costing him a nickel a word and try to figure it out before allowing it had been sent by a drunken lunatic.

Then, having shelled out hard-earned money and putting away the change, Longarm continued on over to the tent show. By now the steam music sounded exciting as well as ear splitting, and kids were yelling inside the big tent as he approached. But first things coming first, Longarm circled around it, trackside, to scout up some roustabouts among the camp of smaller tents, railcars and such. He'd just spotted some gents near Princess Olga's tent when the calliope music blared, some explosive squibs went off inside, and a big white stallion dashed out through a slit in the main tent to cut across his line of vision with a naked lady tied down, faceup, to its back.

Her long dark hair hung down off the white horse's rump to swish in time with its long white tail. Her bare breasts were bouncing pretty good, as well, as she tore out of sight between a big red wagon and another tent. Longarm stared after her with his jaw dropped and his eyes taking in nothing but slowly settling dust. Then he grinned and muttered, "Right. Flesh-colored tights. They call 'em Leo-somethings. But I'll bet she still shocked the shit out of Sheridan."

Still grinning, he went on to join her road manager, Gradey, and another well-dressed dude he didn't know. Gradey grinned back and asked, "Ain't she the bee's knees? The police raided us in Omaha, one time, when her leotard split at the crotch at full gallop. I've asked her not to ride that wild, in French, but will she listen?"

Longarm chuckled and replied, "Just my luck I was in Omaha another time. Are you sure she's all right? That big stud looked like it was bolting, with her in a sort of helpless position."

Gradey nodded but said, "It's supposed to look like that. The Polish henchmen who tie poor Mazeppa down to die a cruel death on the steppes know better than to really tie her helpless. As soon as she's out of sight she just sits up and grabs the stud's main. She'll be back, directly, unless she decides to put some duds on first. That was her grand exit and she knows she looks sort of naked in that leotard, even if nothing really shows. Do you want a pass for tonight's performance, Deputy Long?"

Longarm said, "No, thanks. Soon as I finish here, I aim to saddle up and see if I can meet that army column before it gets in. I just dropped by to warn you about the old geezer who owns the next lot over. He seems to think you're endangering at least one of his tumble-weeds."

Both the other men laughed and Gradey said, "I just had the boys shift the scenery a few feet. This here is Mr. Marcus Dean, the owner of the land we stand on. He beat you here with the timely advice."

As Longarm shook with the more sensible looking

landlord, Dean said, "Poor old Slade is always stirring up trouble, mostly for himself. Sometimes I suspect he must be part Sioux. He goes into a war dance at the sound of a falling penny."

Longarm said, "So I was just told by another resident of your fair city. I understand a lot of folk here in town are sort of scared of the prune-mouthed old fool."

Dean grimaced and said, "Not me. The last time he sued me I got him thrown out of court and stuck him with the bill from my lawyer. He hasn't messed with me since."

Longarm smiled knowingly and said, "He was dumb to mess with a member of the courthouse gang. What about the rumor he has hired guns on his payroll?"

Dean shook his head and said, "I suspect he started that rumor himself. Slade's too cheap to pay a cleaning woman. Lives in a state of trash-white squallor in a soddy on the wrong side of the tracks. I suspect he jerks off on his moneybags every night. For Lord knows he indulges himself in no other pleasures. He don't drink. He don't smoke. He don't even eat right. Buys his bread a day old, cheaper, from the bakery, and tries to beat down the price of beans as well, the poor old miser."

Longarm allowed he'd met Slade's sort before and didn't see what they got out of it, either. Then he said he had to see about saddling up and started to turn away. But then another notion hit him and he turned back to ask, "Hold on, Marcus. Did I hear you say the old rascal lives alone, across the tracks? There ain't all that much in the way of a town that way."

Dean nodded and replied, "Nothing but loading pens and such. Most folk don't like to live downwind of blowing cinders. That's how come it's the wrong side of the tracks. Slade has a little soddy in a draw, just out of range of the falling sparks from passing trains. He thinks someday the land will be valuable."

Longarm said, "It likely will, once Sheridan gets big enough to need both sides of the tracks. But meanwhile, if he's jerking off out there alone, after dark—"

Dean cut in to say, "I follow your drift. But nobody's going to scalp him tonight. We passed along your advice to the sheriff when he got back with his posse. He's got outposts set up on the rises all around town, a mile or more out. Slade's shack ain't half that far, more's the pity."

Longarm nodded and strode off, bemused. As he circled back to the main street he saw that since the show was over a whole herd of men, women and children had burst out of the main tent to get in his way. As he swerved to keep from running down a brace of whining brats and their haggard mothers, Laughing Raven caught up with him. The Crow lawman said, "Wa, that show was funny. Did you see the naked woman on the white horse? She really knows how to ride."

Longarm replied, "That's the only part I saw. She's putting some duds on, now, I hope. I was figuring on heading off that army column. Want to ride along?"

Laughing Raven said, "Sure. I just saw the tent show, and the saloons will be quiet this evening when they do that again. But do you think just the two of us will be able to stop a whole army column? I'm game if you are, but—"

"I just want to steer 'em, not stop 'em," Longarm cut in. "I want 'em stopping over here in town a spell. They may be planning to in any case. But I want to make sure they don't push on to Little Wolf's camp just yet."

By this time they were approaching the livery.

Laughing Raven asked, "Why? The two of us might be able to beat that many long knives with yellow and red legs. I don't think those Cheyenne could do it. Hear me. Once the blue sleeves round up all those renegades all the trouble ought to be over, over, forever."

Longarm waved to the colored hand in the livery doorway and called out, "The agency bay, and this idiot better have a fresh mount, too. He's just being superstitious about horseshoes. So wrangle him a good fast nag and to hell with his odd notions."

Then he turned back to the Crow and said, "I know this Indian trouble *ought* to be over. That's why I aim to put a stop to it. But forever is a long time and our only fair reason to suspect Little Wolf of acting like a wild Indian is that he's a sort of wild Indian. After that, things just don't fit sensible."

He left it at that until they were leading their saddled ponies out to the street to mount up. As they were doing so, a hand from the tent show ran up to them to ask if they knew the way to the sheriff's office. Longarm pointed at the cupola of the county courthouse, just visible up the street, but asked how come the law might be needed down the other way. The roustabout panted, "We can't find Princess Olga! She rode off in the usual manner, but never came back as usual. We've searched all over camp and beyond for her and that half-wild stud. But they just ain't there. Mr. Gradey fears she might not have managed to get loose, or that if she did she wasn't able to control the critter this time. Either way, she has to be somewhere out on the lone prairie with night coming on and nothing but that thin leotard to guard her fair white body!"

Longarm whistled, told the hand to keep running for more help, and told Laughing Raven, "Let's go. I got a line on the way she was headed. I doubt even a spooked stud will cross railroad tracks with all that grass to dash off across until it comes to its senses."

Laughing Raven didn't answer. As the two of them loped down the street and through the tent-show camp, old Gradey had just mounted his own thoroughbred. As he fell in with them at a lope he called out, "Where are we going? Don't those wild Indians live over to the west?"

Longarm replied, on the bounce, "She wasn't tied down to no Indian pony. It would have come back by now if it knew the lay of the land here at all. It's just running with her, and the easy running ought to be southeast, along the same easy grade the railroad picked out. Running horses don't like to cross rail ballast, even with their rider in charge. So we ought to see them pink tights any minute, down this way. The sheriff's set up outposts all around town. So whether she can stop the stud or not, somebody ought to be doing so, any damned minute."

Then they were clear of the siding and railroad installations with a clear view of the rolling range ahead as far as a cut where the rails passed through a rise the easy way. Longarm called out, "I doubt a horse with a mind of its own would pass through that cut, ahead. He's looking for open country."

So they reined to their left to ride up and over the rise and, as they topped it, Gradey moaned, "Oh, Jesus! I can see for miles and there's no sight of her!"

Longarm didn't answer. He was too busy thinking as they tore across the shallow draw and up yet another rise. He and Laughing Raven both knew, as Custer had found out just to their north, how many things could be hidden in the dips between what looked like a clear view to forever. As they topped the next rise he spied a still-smoldering cow-chip fire and some tin cans off to their right. That accounted for the outpost that was supposed to be around here, some damned where. As they loped down the far slope Longarm called out, "We're on the right course. The boys stationed back there must have spotted her and rode after. That sure must be a sudden horse she's stuck aboard and, damn it, the sun ain't fixing to stay up much longer!"

He reined in on the next rise. Only Gradey asked how come. Laughing Raven said, "Hear me. We can see the tops of many rises, many, from up here. What goes down must come up. Even if those other riders haven't caught up with the crazy woman on the white horse, all three of them should top another rise, sooner or later, and then we can head the bad pony off."

Longarm nodded and said, "The big stud figures to keep the lead on two cow ponies carrying more weight. The princess can't weigh as much as a grown man and his saddle, pink tights and all. But where in thunder *are* they? It can't take a bolting horse that long to cross one infernal draw."

Laughing Raven pointed off farther to the east and said, "I think she and her horse are down. See that burrowing owl rising? It is too early for owls to fly, unless something has disturbed them."

Longarm heeled his bay that way at a dead run, letting the others catch up with him as best they could. One horse falling in a grassy draw made sense. Three didn't. Not by accident.

As he bore down on the draw the owl had risen above, he heard the princess before he could see her. Her voice called out in anguish, *"Nyet! Nyet! Mais non. Aux secours! Hilfen!"* So he had his six-gun out as he topped the rise to take in the scene at a glance.

It wasn't pretty, even though the two unkempt white men who'd shot her white stud and spread her on the grass had heard him coming and already leaped off her to run for their own ponies. Longarm shot the farthest one first. The one trying to run with his jeans down around his knees was even easier to drop. Then he tore down into the draw to slide out of his saddle and drop to one knee by the still-screaming gal in pink tights, saying, "Take it easy, Princess. They can't bother you no more and, ah, did they bother you all that much?"

She replied, in Spanish, "By the grace of God this one-piece leotard seemed to confuse them. They must have thought I was really naked, in the heat of the moment. But you got here just in time. Look how they tore my poor leotard!"

He did, but then looked quickly away. She sure was a hairy little thing and her belly button was exposed as well. He put his hot six-gun away and whipped off his tweed coat to wrap it around her just as Gradey and Laughing Raven rode down to join them.

The Indian said, "Wa!" as he read the story with his keen eyes.

Gradey had to ask what had happened. So Longarm said, "Nothing complicated. The uncouth saddle tramps a shorthanded sheriff posted to watch for Indians spotted an apparently naked lady tearing by them aboard a white horse and just acted uncouth. We got here in time to save Wyoming the expense of hanging the bastards. The lady says they never mistreated her all the way."

Gradey said, "Thank God."

But the princess, able to savvy that much English, at least, told them all, in Spanish, to thank the brave Custis Long instead. So Longarm helped her to her feet and told her, "I only did what I had to. I'm sorry about your circus horse. But we've two extra, now. So pick one out to ride and we'd better head back to civilization. The sheriff can clean up here in the morning. This is no place for anyone to be after sundown."

But Laughing Raven said, "Hear me. This is no place to be right now! We'd better make our stand on that next rise. It is higher."

Longarm didn't argue. He'd already heard the thunder of pony hooves, a heap of 'em, coming fast. So he just forked himself into the saddle, scooped up Princess Olga, and chased Laughing Raven up the next ridge, calling out to Gradey, "Move your fool ass, damn it!"

All three of them made the top of the next rise. It was still close. Gradey went down with his own mount when it caught an arrow meant for him. Longarm and Laughing Raven had already spilled their own ponies flat in the grass with the bewildered Russian gal between them, as safe as it was possible to get in such disgusting surroundings. As Gradey rolled over his own downed thoroughbred to join them in the all-too-low fort of horseflesh, he gasped, "I don't understand! Where did all those Indians come from?"

Longarm was too busy to answer stupid questions. His agency bay took an arrow and flinched just as he had a bead on a son of a bitch painted solid black with yellow spots aboard a pony painted almost as wild. There were about a dozen and a half of them. Some painted even wilder, riding in a circle, just out of range as they loped up and down through the draws to north and south, yelling fit to bust and pegging arrows high and thank God mostly wide. The range didn't discourage Laughing Raven from blasting away with his own saddle gun. But as he paused to reload, Longarm told him, "Save your rapid fire for when they get up the nerve to move in. Can't you see they're trying to make us waste all our ammo before they do?"

Laughing Raven must have seen he was out of their range as well, or maybe he was just fighting mad as he rose from behind his livery nag's arrow-studded belly to call out, in the English Crow and Cheyenne had to use against one another, "Hear me! You are cowards, cowards! You still suck your mothers when no real men will let you suck them! You eat dog shit because a man's shit would be too rich for you! If you don't want to fight why don't you go frighten some children with your coyote calls?"

Longarm was glad Princess Olga didn't savvy English. One of the rascals Laughing Raven was taunting must have. Longarm had to cuss him, too, as he rode past them, seated backwards, to give them a very rude hand sign one didn't have to be Indian to savvy. He told the big Crow, "Simmer down and take cover, damn it. There's no telling where a really lucky shot might wind up. Do you read these boys as Contraries, too?"

Laughing Raven remained on his feet as he growled, "They have to be. I don't like any Cheyenne, but most of them fight more like men than this bunch. Their medicine paint is crazy, too. Only a Contrary would paint his face as a mourning woman if he was out for the joy of counting coup."

Then the angry Crow shook his fist and called out, "Hear me! You are all crazy, crazy! You are not even children of Wakan-Tonka! You are followers of the crazy spirits! Do you think the new songs of that crazy Paiute, Wovoka, are stronger than the old songs? Do you think his new ghost dances will bring back the

154

Shining Times or that his medicine shirts will really stop bullets? Come closer, little brothers! Let us see how good your crazy new medicine is! I promise I will only aim at your shirts! Let us see what a man who is content with Wakan-Tonka can do to little girls with contrary medicine!"

There were no takers and, damn it, the sun was getting mighty low. Longarm could no longer make out the flashing stripes of paint as riders whipped between him and the ominously red sun just above the black distant mountains. They seemed to be maintaining that same damned range. But old Norma had told him this special Winchester she'd given him was long barreled with range in mind. So he decided he'd best find out before it got too dark to see the infernal sights.

He drew a bead on a feather-headed son of a bitch riding backwards up out of the draw to his right. He aimed at the pony as the easier target and, sure enough, sent it ass-over-teakettle with his first shot!

That inspired him to aim next time at the rider, and as his man bit the dust he downed another pony. Then Laughing Raven leaped clean over him from behind to dash out in the open with his eight-inch bowie glittering wickedly red, already, in the sunset.

Longarm bawled, "Get back here, you damned fool!" even as he trained his smoking muzzle to cover the crazy Crow. But the Contraries had noticed how far that special Winchester carried, by now, and their circle widened a heap more as Laughing Raven made it unscathed to the fallen rider, hunkered down for just one grisly moment, and rose to shake a bloody scalp at them, yelling, "I count coup! See your brother's hair in my hand, you woman-hearts? What are you going to do about it? What are you going to tell his women when they ask how you avenged him? Don't *yell* at me, you killers of women and old men! I have dogs back home who bark braver than you! Come fight me! I am ready, ready! In the open, like a man, you piss-drinking spawn of fly maggots!"

Then, as far as Longarm could see by such tricky light, the worked-up Crow was alone out there. It must have looked that way to Laughing Raven, too. He strode proudly back to them, saying, "Damn. I was in the mood for a good fight, too. Do you think I overdid it? I didn't want to scare them all away."

Longarm laughed and said, "You sure scared *me*. Would you come back in here, now? It's almost dark, we ain't got beans to ride, and Lord only knows whether the sounds of gunplay carried far enough to do us any good."

The tall Indian stood on a dead pony's rump for a better view before he said, "Wa, I thought I saw something flash on a rise to the northeast. It looks like an army gúidon. Maybe four miles out. Do you want this scalp? I can't count coup on a man you dropped if it wasn't really my teasing that drove those cowards away."

Longarm replied he had no house-room for bloody scalps. So Laughing Raven tossed it out on the grass. By this time Princess Olga was asking more questions than her citified road manager knew the answers to. So Longarm sat up to assure her in Spanish that it was over, explaining, "The soldados we've been expecting must have heard the shooting and the Indians saw their flag before we did. It takes brave men of any color to take on the U.S. Army on an open field, and those Contraries didn't seem all that brave to begin with." He didn't think she wanted to hear, so he switched to Eng-

156

lish to tell Gradey and Laughing Raven, "They'd have had us, had they possessed any balls. The lady here had no weapons at all and, no offense, that one six-gun under your coat wouldn't have stopped more than a few. Considering how they paint their hides, they sure were careful of the same. Custer would still be around if dropping just one warrior stopped a war party, as a rule."

Laughing Raven said, "They were sissies, even for Cheyenne."

To which Longarm replied, "I just said that. So how come they've been acting so scary?"

Chapter 11

Things got a lot brighter when the advance guard of mounted troopers rode in, even though the sunset kept getting darker. For the tall lean cavalry captain in the lead wore a familiar face as well as a puzzled smile. He called out, "I might have known it was you, Longarm. What's up?"

Longarm strode to meet the officer as the latter dismounted. The tall deputy told the tall captain, "Nothing much up. One of them Contraries you may have heard about *down*." Then he turned to his companions to announce, "For once the War Department did something right. I want you all to meet my old pal, Matt Kincaid. He's spilled more hostiles than me in his time. But that's only because he's had more practice. They hardly ever send him after wild white men."

As the officer shook with everyone but the princess —an officer and gentleman knowing he should kiss a lady's hand when she held it out like that—Longarm filled him in on their recent misadventures. Kincaid wanted a look at the dead Contrary. So they left the more delicate Princess Olga in the keeping of her road manager and the U.S. Army as they moved out afoot for a look-see.

Kincaid rolled the body on its back with his boot to

stare down soberly and say, "Ugly squint-eyed cuss, wasn't he? How come he was scalped? I hope you know the government frowns on such war trophies, pard."

Longarm said, "My Crow sidekick just done it to rile his pals. He never kept the scalp and you can see I'd already put some .44-40 in the idiot's head."

The officer grimaced and said, "Between the two of you and all that yellow paint, he'd sure have a time getting a lady to dance with him, if he was still able to dance. Shouldn't he have at least some blue streaks on him, if he was Cheyenne?"

Longarm nodded but said, "The Contrary Lodge don't seem to hold with formality, Matt. They come at us painted all colors of the rainbow, some of 'em riding backwards. They fought us all contrary, too. Yellow livered or not, at least some of 'em was supposed to call back insults when Laughing Raven even mentioned their mothers. He did so in English, of course. That princess with us don't savvy the lingo."

Kincaid said, "I was just about to ask about the lady with your party. Is she really naked under that old coat of yours?"

Longarm laughed and said, "Pink tights. Fortunately my coattails hang way down past the important rips in her circus outfit."

They left the corpse to whoever or whatever might have better use for that much dead meat and Longarm explained the princess to the officer, as well, by the time they'd rejoined her and the others. Kincaid said the dead white men no soldier had ever laid eyes on could hardly be of interest to the War Department, and added, "I'd better get you all safely into Sheridan before we go have that talk with Little Wolf. I fear we're going to have to ride double on at least five army mounts."

Longarm agreed and, being no fool, made sure he and Princess Olga rode the same cavalry pony vacated by a trooper who got to ride double with someone a lot less pretty. She'd have looked scandalous enough riding sidesaddle in those pink tights But she forked one naked-looking leg over to ride pillion behind Longarm, and the troopers had been disciplined well enough by Kincaid not to whistle, albeit more than one meant to write home about how wild the wild West really was.

Once they were all headed right in the gathering dusk, Longarm reined in beside the officer in the lead to say, "I'd like you to study on riding Little Wolf down, before you do it, Matt. I do take it you're in command here."

Kincaid said, "You take it wrong. I'm serving under a Major Wimbourne, in command of the whole column. By now he'll be in town ahead of us. My own troop and I were only sent out of the way to see what all that shooting was about. Are you sure the lady you're riding with doesn't speak English?"

Longarm told the officer he was pretty sure. So Kincaid told him, "The major is an asshole of the old school. Made his oak leaves back East, shining shoes in Washington with his tongue, and so now that Mister Lo has been whipped he's out here to win at least one ribbon as an Old Indian Fighter. I've already told him Little Wolf never led a big band to begin with. Wait until you see the breech-loading field guns he brought along, anyway."

Longarm didn't answer as he hauled out a cheroot. The Russian gal clinging to him from behind said she could use a smoke, too, "Por favor." So as they went through the contortions of getting two smokes going aboard one pony, Kincaid asked, "Not that it'll do any good, but what's the story on Little Wolf? He *is* on the books as a *renegade,* you know."

Longarm waited until he and the princess were puffing a mite more serenely before he explained, "A scared old renegade whose only real crime is wanting to be left the hell alone. Would it really bring down the white world, entire, if one small band of Cheyenne was allowed to just go on acting natural, Matt?"

Kincaid said dubiously, "It might be sort of hard on the hair of at least a few white folk. How many deaths and injuries have they racked up so far?"

Longarm shrugged and said, "I'd agree one was too many. But old Little Wolf's been over in them foothills a good two years and, so far, the only white he ever tried to kill was me."

Kincaid laughed and said, "You sure have a forgiving nature."

But Longarm insisted, "Understanding, you mean. He just tried to keep me from giving away his position, with army columns like your own in mind. I ain't sure Little Wolf is really behind all this Contrary riding. Where in the Constitution does it say it's fair to punish one man for another man's crime?"

Kincaid replied soberly, "The Constitution wasn't written with the rights of renegades in mind, Longarm. But I'm listening and I may even be able to get the major to listen, if you have someone else in mind for us to ride down."

Longarm had been afraid Kincaid would ask something like that. The cuss had been through college, even before he'd learned so much about Indians in the field, ever since. Longarm tried, "The Crow lawman with me agrees them Contrary riders make no sense as Little Wolf's followers. If you were a beaten but still proud chief, trying to hang on to one last bitty hunting ground and hoping nobody knew where you were, would you advertise your current address by sending out war parties to stir things up?"

Kincaid said, "They sure stirred things up. I'm anxious to settle this before the first fall blizzards hit, too. Hunting hostiles across snow may be easier, but it sure can get uncomfortable to all concerned. If those Cheyenne don't really want to fight us we can have 'em back at Fort Reno, where they belong, before it gets too cold to herd them."

Longarm said flatly, "Little Wolf doesn't want to go back to Fort Reno. He'll fight you. Even if it means they all go under, and there's a heap of women and kids in that camp, damn it."

Kincaid sighed and said, "I wish there was a way of keeping women and children out of wars, too. But most Indians go in for big families and they're as careless as the Mexican Army when it comes to having them tagging along. Do you remember that one big Shoshone camp we hit that time near the South Pass?"

Longarm growled, "I've been trying to forget it ever since. You boys in blue can forget it if you want me to scout for you again."

Kincaid said, "The Tongue River is on our ordnance map. You don't have to show us the way if you don't want to. I don't want you riding ahead to warn Little Wolf, either. I mean that. I know you of old and I like you, Longarm. But you have my word I'll charge you with High Treason if you ever pull a stunt like that again."

Longarm smiled sheepishly and said, "Hell, Matt, you know them Arapaho I tipped off that time were innocent bystanders."

But the more poker-faced captain insisted, "That was for us to judge and, even if you were right, that one time, Little Wolf stands convicted as a renegade by his own mouth. Never chase an Indian agent away with war whoops if you want the Great White Father fond of you. If we can round 'em up alive we will. But round 'em up we shall. Orders are orders, and if you don't want to help us, stay out."

Longarm could see the army didn't want to argue. Meanwhile Princess Olga was poking at his floating ribs and fussing at him about something. So, finding it easier to think in either English or Spanish at the same time, Longarm dropped back to ask her in Spanish what was eating her. She asked if they couldn't go faster, explaining, "By now my clowns have tumbled themselves to sheer exhaustion and the bears of Boyer Boris only know so many tricks."

Longarm laughed incredulously and said, "I know the show must go on. But you just said you have other acts to entertain the crowd, and haven't you had enough excitement for one day?"

She sighed and said, "Mazeppa may have been overdoing it. I don't know what got into that poor horse. But my trusty rosin-backs are waiting for my grand entrance and I am used to going on with bruises and aching bones. We promised the good people of Sheridan an afternoon and evening show. I can't fail my public!"

Longarm was tempted to tell her it would be easy. But he liked the gal's spunk. So he caught up with the captain again and said, "This little lady says she'd like to get into town, now. Where did you boys pick up these nags, a glue factory?"

Matt Kincaid had a boyish streak of his own when he didn't have to look strict. So he raised his right gauntlet

163

and called out, "In column. . . . For'd. . . . Hyohhhh!" and they were charging to town at a pace that surely would have spilled the princess if she didn't know how to ride so well without stirrups.

Her road manager, Gradey, did fall off the mount he was riding with Laughing Raven. But it worked out all right when the disgusted Crow hauled him back aboard by the collar and carried Gradey in the rest of the way across the saddle like a mighty noisy corpse.

Once they'd reached the tent-show grounds the princess dropped off and ran for her dressing tent without so much as an adios to anybody. Laughing Raven spilled Gradey to the ground like a feed sack and rode to join Longarm and the captain, asking where they had to go, now. Kincaid said he and his men had to report in to their C.O. at the hotel he was using as his field headquarters. Longarm and the Indian headed for the sheriff's office to report the death of his two unmannerly deputies.

The sheriff didn't seem to care. He was a gruff old cuss who said they could call him Pappy Cohen. He said, "I'm glad you saved a female guest of my county a raping, Longarm. I confess I just assigned them saddle tramps to that outpost because I'm shorthanded when it comes to forming a circle around the entire city. I'll send the morgue wagon out to pick 'em up as soon as my fool deputy comes back. I sent him to get me some smokes and I suspect he's taking in that tent show."

Longarm handed Cohen a couple of extra cheroots as he said, "I'd hold off until daybreak if I were you, Pappy. I was just getting to the war party me and Laughing Raven, here, ran into shortly thereafter."

Cohen lit a smoke and listened sharp until Longarm had him up to date on the brush with the Contraries.

Then he nodded soberly and said, "Well, it don't sound tidy, according to my faith. But I don't think either Mason or Greenwood were Jewish. So it won't hurt if they lie in state overnight or, hell, 'til after the army rounds up them red rascals. You say you gunned them no more than a mile southeast of where I told them they were supposed to stay put?"

Longarm nodded and explained, "I doubt they expected to spy a naked lady riding past so tempting. According to her, she'd untied herself and sat up to rein in long before she got out so far. But her mount was supposed to be mane-trained, and as things turned out, she couldn't even slow it down that way. She thinks, and I agree, it must have eaten some loco weed."

The older sheriff nodded but said, "Could have been turpentine under its tail, too. You learn about such practical jokes when you ride as the only Jewish kid on a Texas trail drive. Some good old boys damned near busted my neck that way one time. Had to gun my poor pony to keep from going over a cliff with it. Damn near had to gun two Texans, later. But they were willing to fistfight, and after that I got along all right with the outfit."

Longarm smiled thinly and said he recalled initiation into the cattle industry, right after the war. Then he frowned thoughtfully and mused, "Hmm, any number of folk could have patted that stud on the ass with a hand wet with anything stingy in the confusion of her dramatic act inside the tent. It's a long shot. But I'd better warn Princess Olga, next time I see her, that someone in her outfit could have a nasty sense of humor, or a hankering to take her place as the star."

They jawed and smoked some more. Then Longarm and Laughing Raven had to return their borrowed cavalry mounts to the cavalry. It was obvious Major Wimbourne wasn't fixing on night-fighting Indians. Longarm hailed one of the troopers on the street who still looked sober and asked which hotel his G.H.Q. was set up in. When the trooper told him it was the Grand Paris Hotel, Longarm groaned, turned to Laughing Raven, and said, "I have a favor to ask, pard. I'd like to get down and let you carry both these ponies back to Captain Kincaid for us."

The Indian said, "I will do it, then. But why do you want to avoid the army after all the time we just spent with them?"

Longarm said, "I ain't ducking the army. I'm ducking a lady who works at that hotel. In a moment of weakness, the last time I was in town, I promised I'd look her up if ever I passed this way again."

The big Crow grinned knowingly, said he had moments of such weakness as well, and led Longarm's mount on as soon as its saddle was empty.

Longarm strode on down to the Western Union, first. Inside he not only found replies to some wires he'd sent but a wire he dreaded as well. Old Billy Vail had wired him:

ARE YOU STILL THERE QUESTION MARK IF SO GET YOUR DELETED BY WESTERN UNION BACK TO DENVER STOP MARSHAL VAIL REPEAT MARSHAL AND ADD BOSS

Longarm tossed it in the wastebasket and put the others in a side pocket of a coat that still smelled a lot like a Russian gal's perfumed armpits. There didn't seem to be any trains bound for Denver leaving right now in any case. But he knew Vail was going to grill him about that. So he headed for the railroad shack by the open loading platform they used as a general depot and asked the old coot inside for a timetable.

The old coot said he didn't have any infernal timetable if they were talking about printed material. But when Longarm flashed his federal badge and allowed it might be important, the old coot reached in a drawer, drew out a sheaf of carbon papers, and gave them to Longarm, saying, "Here. We can spare you last week's dispatch flimsies, since this ain't last week. Freights and such ran any damned time there's a clear track and a place to go. But passenger varnishes generally run about the same time day-by-day. It's a bother, but it saves folk calling us names as they wait for their damned old trains."

Longarm thanked him and stuffed the onionskins in with the rest of his reading material, for later. Then he strode on down to the tent show. He asked the pretty young gal in the ticket window how much he owed her. But she said she knew who he was and not to be silly. So he ticked his hat brim at her and went on in.

He found a place to stand, all the seats being filled with local folk and twice as many kids, and saw Princess Olga was in the middle of her grand finale. It sure was grand. For as if to make up for not letting them see her play Mazeppa, or even admire her pink tights, old Olga was tearing around the ring, facing backwards in a sort of cossack coat, no pants, with a foot on each of two white horses' rumps. She likely got a buy on big white horses. Another tent-show lady he remembered fondly had once told him they were called rosin-backs because they spread powdered rosin on their backs to keep the performer's feet from slipping on sweaty horse-hide. Princess Olga was still one hell of a horsewoman, though.

She waved to him as she tore past. Then she got both feet planted on one horse, which looked easier, and did a black flip across to the other, which didn't. As the crowd went wild she rode backwards out that same slit, blowing kisses to them all.

Recalling what had happened the last time she'd dashed off on horseback that way, Longarm ducked out and circled after her. But this time he found her near her private tent, on foot, and feeding the big rosin-back a treat as two roustabouts ran over to take charge of it. As Longarm joined them the princess told him she'd hoped he'd join her after the show because they had a lot to talk about. Longarm said he might have something to tell her, as well. But she led him inside her tent and sat him down on a cot near one of those big brass Russian teapots as she explained she had to go over some figures with her hired help and road manager before she could devote her full attention to him. Then she damn it left him there alone without even saying if it was all right to smoke in her tent or not.

He decided not to. The luxurious but modest-sized tent had no windows to open, and he figured a gal who'd sprayed that much expensive smelling rose perfume all over her stuff liked the reek of roses better than she might three-for-a-nickel tobacco smoke. So he chewed on an unlit cheroot instead until, no more than a million years later, she came back.

She asked him not to look as she swapped her cossack coat for a cotton robe, too white to be anything but clean, and let him watch as she sat at a bitty table across the tent to cold-cream her makeup off. They could talk face-to-face in her table mirror. So he told her Sheriff

Cohen's suspicions about turpentine. She wrinkled her nose and said that sounded horrid, but that she already had the answer, and it was just a mistake. She said she blamed herself, because she should have been paying more attention to the white horse they were lashing her to as a Polish man called Mazeppa. They'd used the wrong horse. A green hand had mixed up white rosin-backs in the hurry of the moment and, naturally, a critter trained to simply run had simply run when it found itself outside the ring it was trained to run in. It hadn't been trained to stop when anyone pulled its mane because lots of tricks involved hanging on to the mane at a gallop. Those would-be rapists hadn't done a thing to slow the poor brute down as they'd chased after her, yelling dirty until they'd shot it. So, in sum, she said, she was out one horse and that was the end of it.

He stared at her mirrored face and pondered aloud, "Mistakes like that can still get one killed. How many inexperienced helpers might you have in your pago, Princesa?"

She sighed and said, "You should ask how many of them really know the business. Most of my featured performers have been on the road with me some time. It is hard to keep less glamorous help. They come and they go. It seems everyone wants to run away with the circus, but nobody wants to drive stakes on a cold gray morning. Fortunately, I am able to pay almost as much as a young man with a love of travel might make as a vaquero. So, as I just said, they come and they go."

He said, "It might be interesting to see who's been coming and going, lately. A traveling tent show would make a neat hideout. Do you have a roster of all the names tearing cross-country with your outfit, Princesa?"

She dabbed at the last of her eyebrow blackening as

she told him her road manager surely would, in the pay wagon. Then she leaned back to face him soberly, in the mirror, as she said, "There. Now I have no secrets from you at all, thanks to the way they tore my leotard. What do you think of this old girl, now?"

He could see she might be even older than thirty and change, albeit still a mighty handsome woman. He knew she didn't want to hear that. So he said, "It's just as well women aren't allowed to vote. You'd never pass for twenty-one if you tried to, next month."

She turned on her stool with a radiant smile to confide, "I am almost forty. I think it must be my Tatar blood that keeps my skin from wrinkling. But, honestly, do you really think I am still desirable?"

He shot her a sheepish grin and said, "If you were not such a grand lady and I wasn't trying to be a gentleman, I'd just show you how desirable I found you, and you know it."

So she rose, allowing her robe to fall open but trimming the lamp just as he was taking in all the charms he hadn't seen before, as she purred softly, "Then show me."

So he did. After they'd damned near busted through her cot she agreed it might be safer doing it naked on the Persian rug spread across the dry grass of the lot. He had no trouble recalling the quick glimpse he'd had of all her naked charms, as he rolled all over them in passion. For the little Russian spitfire was so firm from all that hard riding that even her sweet breasts felt muscular.

For a gal who called herself a princess, even in fun, old Olga seemed to like it down-home and natural. He didn't mind at all. They both could have used a bath, and a healthy man didn't need any naughty trimmings to

170

keep him inspired aboard a strong, hot-loving gal who never stopped moving, even between times. But by the time they'd climaxed to the point of losing count, she told him they were fixing to overturn her makeup table, and asked if he'd like to go back aboard the cot and have some tea and at least a short break.

He laughed and agreed he'd try anything that didn't hurt. So they wound up lolling together on the cot, naked as jays and not minding that, at all, as they sipped tea from glasses. The tea was strong and natural as it came out a spigot in her samovar. She placed a sugar cube between her sweet lips and sucked tea through it. She said that was how they did it in the old country and suggested he try it. He said he liked his tea the way it was. It was hard to talk, even in simple Spanish, to a Russian lady with her mouth puckered on a sugar cube. But they managed to talk about this and that, some of it even interesting, before she finished her refreshment, saw he'd finished his, and dragged him down to the rug to get on top this time, with the lamp burning. He smiled up at her and told her she sure knew how to handle a stud, whether it ran on four legs or just two. She smiled back down at him to say, "Thank you. I enjoy riding this way, better. I try to behave myself on the road, but you are so handsome, and you did save my life and, well, maybe it is just my Tatar blood."

He said, "You keep saying that and you have the advantage on me about such matters. Might a Tatar be something like a cossack?"

She laughed and replied, "Such an odd time to be having such a conversation. Tatars are much wilder than cossacks. They would be more like Huns, I think. Savage tribesmen from the eastern steppes, before we converted those we did not have to kill. My maternal grandmother was said to be pure Tatar. I must get my passion and way with horses from her."

Longarm tore his gaze from her bouncing breasts in order to study her pretty face harder as he said, "That makes you a quarter-breed, then. It's funny, but you don't look Chinese."

She giggled and asked, "Oh, didn't you notice the way I am built between my legs? I think it shows, just a little, in my cheekbones. The skulls of most pure Georgians are just sort of, well, ordinary. Do you really find me attractive? You don't mind my looking just a bit Oriental?"

He didn't see how in thunder a man in his present position could do any more to assure a gal he liked her. So he rolled her on her back to see if he could convince her that way. Apparently he could. For the next time he made her come, pounding her like hell, it seemed to knock her clean out.

He made sure she was only sleeping off the effects of the exciting times she'd just been through, and then got out of there before she could wake up again and ruin his back entire. Any other time he might not have minded, but now that things were starting to fit together he knew he'd need all his strength and wits about him in the near future.

Chapter 12

Longarm caught up with Captain Matt Kincaid at daybreak, in the dining room at the Grand Paris Hotel. There were times a man just had to risk a waitress cussing him. Longarm sat down across the breakfast table from Kincaid, but said, "Finish your fool eggs. I ain't got time. I'm fixing to make some mass arrests and my guns only carry so many bullets. Where's that major of yours, if we have to clear it with him, first."

Kincaid went on sedately eating eggs as he replied, "I doubt the major will be out of bed this side of noon. He was last seen turning in, upstairs, with a fifth of bourbon and a hotel waitress with a homely face and a truely lovely behind. But, I warn you, that only lets Little Wolf off until this afternoon."

Longarm grinned and said, "If we're talking about the same waitress, your C.O. won't get off before she has to come on duty this evening. But, what the hell, they'll issue him that pretty red and blue ribbon just for riding this far. We don't have to worry about Little Wolf's band no more, Matt."

Kincaid scowled, reached for his coffee cup, and said, "Damn it, Longarm. I thought we'd settled that last night. *Some* damned Indians have *hair* to pay for in

173

these parts, and those Cheyenne are the only ones within miles!"

Longarm saw it might take some convincing, so he let Kincaid go on eating as he said, "You're both right and wrong. Those wild-acting contrary-painted rascals have done all the damage to life and property all up and down the Burlington line of late. But keep in mind they've never hit more than a few miles from the tracks. Then get set for me to tell you I don't think they could be real Indians."

Kincaid put down his coffee to just stare at him. So Longarm nodded and said, "I have it on good authority that lots of Russian folk have Tatar blood. A Tatar is something like a Chinee, only they look as much like our own Indians. They don't *all* have to be Russian Tatars, of course. An unusual tooth here and high cheek bones under war paint and body stain there could be enough to confuse a fool like me."

Kincaid said, "You're confusing me while you're at it. That so-called Princess Olga did have an unusual set of cheekbones, as I recall. But are you accusing her and her show folk of all those raids?"

Longarm shook his head and said, "Pretty little Olga doesn't speak English and, half the time, doesn't know where she *is*. I just went over some railroad manifests, though. Would you call it sensible to run a special train all up and down the same rail line, willy-nilly but often near the scene of a Contrary raid, if you were in show business for sensible profit, Matt?"

Kincaid agreed he would not, but asked for more proof than just possible before he skipped the waffles he'd ordered as well.

Longarm said, "You know Plains Indians as well or better than me, Matt. That's maybe why you're still so

174

healthy. They were never just wild. They always had some *plan* in mind, even if it was no more than stealing ponies or getting laid. So I've been trying to figure a motive. I told why it would have been dumb for Little Wolf to send out them Contraries. Some young men he sent out after me may or may not have hit the Rocking Seven a few nights ago for ponies. It works either way. But most of the attacks have been a heap less sensible. They just hit here and there, always within easy reach of a railroad siding, and worse yet, passing on easy targets most untested braves might find more tempting. There's an old miser named Slade, lives alone just outside town with nothing to protect him but moneybags. Indians know what money is. Red Cloud asked for a cash settlement that time in the Black Hills, remember?"

Kincaid nodded grim-lipped and said, "They should have given it to him. Terry's summer in the field cost the taxpayers more, in the end. Tell me more about your mysterious old miser."

Longarm said, "Nothing to tell. He's likely just old and loco en la cabeza. Sorry about that, I've been talking Spanish half the night. Old Slade ain't smart or popular enough to mastermind anything half as dirty. They've left him alone for the simple reason that there's no gain in hitting him and, of course, he *does* make a dandy *suspect,* once anyone wises up a mite."

Kincaid asked what motives Longarm had connected to the other raids across three counties, in that case. So Longarm said, "The main motive was to get you right here, waiting on waffles and an attack on them hold-out Cheyenne. Most of the raids were just easy raids, with nobody all that shot up on either side. But I just got a wire from Land Management and I find it interesting that a squaw-man called Watkins had just filed a federal

175

claim on land and water between here and the Tongue River. Don't you?"

Kincaid said, "I'm not sure. Land grab? What on earth would Princess Olga want to do that for? She doesn't seem interested in staying put long enough to prove a claim, and is she even a U.S. citizen?"

"I doubt it," Longarm said. "You got to speak English, at least. Her road manager, Gradey, is as American as we are, and it's been him booking the show so dumb, back and forth, and hiring on hands the princess can't even talk to. But, just like her, Gradey is a wandering showman, and I doubt he's interested in even rich cattle range and water rights. So what if he was working for someone more local? I can't come up with a soul who'd find it half as easy as a gent with the use of a private train and all the theatrical makeup and props he wanted to order on the sly."

Kincaid said, "Hmmm! Say a dozen-odd tent-show hands sort of wandered off, with show stock, shod or unshod, to turn into a war band out in open country and then turn back to white men before they drifted back and simply boarded the train before one posse rider showed up to track them—"

Longarm cut in to say, "Sheriff Cohen's going to be pleased to learn he wasn't outsmarted by real Indians as he chased the same all over creation to no avail. It's simple to outride any posse aboard a train whilst they're scouting for pony tracks, and leave us not forget not one unguarded telegraph pole or length of railroad track was ever damaged by those so-called bloodthirsty savages."

Kincaid nodded but asked, "What about the attack on Gradey as well as you, the princess and Laughing Raven? Someone out to change places with the leader of the gang?"

Longarm shook his head and said, "Mistaken identity. They had no call to expect their boss way out on the prairie he'd sent them to raise more hell on. As soon as they closed in enough to see who was with us, they just put on a show, hoping we'd report the attack and alibi Gradey at the same time. I messed 'em up by firing an unusual Winchester. They'd no doubt taken it for a regular one when I rode past 'em in town more than once."

He reached thoughtfully for one of the fresh cheroots he'd bought that morning and lit up before he added, "I lost my old saddle out yonder as well. Maybe when this is all over I'll be able to recover all my possibles. I'd sure miss my old saddle. How long does it take to cook waffles, for God's sake?"

Kincaid folded his napkin and said, "Screw the waffles. I'd say it's about time we had a talk with Mr. Gradey. How many guns do you think you'll need to back your play, pard?"

Longarm rose from the table with the grim-faced officer, saying, "Hard to say. He has to be in cahoots with at least two dozen so-called roustabouts. Too many might be better than too few."

Kincaid said, "I'll round up a couple of squads, then."

But Longarm said, "Hold on. Let's study on this. Most of them show folk figure to be innocent foreigners, and there could be hell to pay if the real bastards spied half a platoon of yellow legs advancing on 'em all at once. The camp should be calm this early before the noon day show. What say we just sort of drift in, like curious cusses looking to pet a bear or flirt with a showgal?"

Kincaid agreed. So a few minutes later Longarm strode on to the tent-show grounds, alone, and when he

177

spied Gradey near the tracks, talking to some shabbier dressed workers, he waved and went over to join them. He said, "Morning. I don't see the boss-lady about."

To which Gradey answered, "She's not up, yet. She seems to have had a rough night. Is there anything *I* can do for you, Deputy?"

It might have seemed obvious, had he craned his neck to see where in thunder that damned Kincaid and his men might be. So he just shrugged and said, "Oh, nothing in particular. Just call me a curious cuss by nature."

"Curious about what?" growled one of the roustabouts, who seemed to feel the need of a gun on his hip as well as the bib overalls he had on. Gradey shot him a shushing look. But the tough's guilty conscience inspired him to mutter, "He knows."

They were all wearing guns, come to study on it, as they all swung to scowl at him at once. He made it five against one, counting Gradey, who surely had that same S&W under his coat.

Longarm had five rounds in the wheel. But that didn't worry him as much as the fact that there had to be more than four of the sons of bitches playing Indian when their boss-lady wasn't looking. Longarm tried, "I'm missing something, here, gents. Did I just bust up a crap game or something?"

Gradey sighed and said, "Damn it, Nate. I told you to make sure you used plenty of cold cream," and the one with just a hint of brown greasepaint in the corners of his nose went for his gun without even answering.

It was close. Longarm had his gun out and had two of them on the way down before another shot his hat off. But old Gradey had a bead on Longarm's back just as an Army .45 slug smacked into the treacherous road manager's skull and blew his eyeballs out to the end of thier stalks.

After that it got really noisy. Matt Kincaid was atop the flatbed railcar he'd been hunkered behind to shout orders at everyone as they mostly pegged shots at one another. The orders were for anyone who didn't want to die to hit the grass, spread out and empty-handed. Some did and some just ran in circles, screaming, male and female, while the more serious crooks all over camp dove from cover to cover, searching for a target in all that smoke. But old Matt had had his troopers circle all about before moving in, and so no matter where a rascal wanted to fire from, some war-whooping trooper had a bead on his ass-end, and used it. Old Matt Kincaid had trained his boys to fight wilder Indians than these fake ones.

So it was over in minutes, which was just as well. For Princess Olga came running through the smoke at Longarm in her open robe, threw her half-naked self against him, and wailed, "What is this? Another Indian attack? Oh, when will it ever end, *querido*?"

He patted her back with the hand he didn't have a smoking gun in and soothed, "It just ended. Gradey was acting two-faced and no doubt doctoring the books as well. You and your decent friends are going to be all right and maybe richer, once you find a less dishonest manager."

Matt Kincaid dropped off the wagon bed to come and join them, grinning like a mean little kid. He said, "That one in the dude outfit *had* you, Longarm."

To which Longarm could only reply, "Thanks. I hope you'll remember the one I shot off *your* back as well, just after. I sure wish we could have taken Gradey in a more conversational condition, though. Confession is good for the soul and proving the rest may be tougher."

By this time half of Sheridan, including both the town and county law, had come running toward the sounds of gunplay to see what all the noise had been about. The old town law, to his credit, put his deputies right to work at keeping the crowd back lest they trip over bodies. Longarm was trying to reload with old Olga still wrapped around him when Pappy Cohen and Marcus Dean, the owner of this battlefield, joined them. The sheriff whistled softly as he gazed about at the carnage, there being one trooper down but still alive with a comrade helping him, and exactly nineteen crooks who needed no medical assistance at all. Cohen said, "All right. I'm listening." So Longarm made it terse but complete enough for the sheriff to grasp. When he'd finished the sheriff said, "Well, I never," and the city-council member and lawful owner of all this blood-soaked grass said, "Good Lord. To think I let them use this lot, free, as a base of operations! Do you have any idea why they were doing it, Deputy?"

Longarm said, "Sure, they were hired to sow fear and confusion far and wide. After that, things get more murky and hard to prove. With both the sheriff, here, and the town law chasing fake Contraries where they weren't, it even struck bank robbers as a good time to hit town. But I still suspect the main motive of the mastermind was luring the army this way. Sorry, Matt, but facts are facts and you boys were suckered."

As if to prove they weren't completely useless, a cavalry sergeant came up to Matt Kincaid with a war club and a quiver of arrows to salute and say, "Trooper Murphy just found these in one of the work wagons, sir. We're still searching for other such gear, as you ordered."

180

Kincaid said to put all the fake Indian gear they found in one place, for now, and added, "That war club's not Cheyenne. Looks more like Comanche workmanship to me."

Longarm said, "The arrows are a mishmash, too. Hold on." He spoke a few words in Spanish with the Russian gal clinging to him and said, "There you go, Matt. She says her show's played Texas and lots of other places as Gradey zigzagged. They must have been planning all summer, knowing late fall would be the best time to wind things up. Gradey never had to beg, borrow or steal his weaponry from unreconstructed Indians. Such mementos can be picked up for a song all over the west, with genuine clay pots and Navajo jewelry if you want to spend more."

He glanced down at the fortunately facedown corpse of the treacherous road manager to add, "He could use the makeup the princess here bought for her honest clowns at no cost to him at all. White men are allowed to own buckskin jackets and such as long as they wear pants with 'em, most of the time. They used some of the work horses, but likely stole most of the stock they rode. Nobody but Gradey and whoever he hired as wranglers paid all that much attention to the poor lady's remuda. I don't think they switched rosin-backs on her that time on purpose. She was too good a cover for Gradey. But wranglers who know what they're doing are more apt to hold a steady job than go wrong."

Sheriff Cohen nodded impatiently and said, "Sure, sure, I see what this gent with his eyes and brains blowed out was up to. I'm mad as hell about all the riding he put me and the boys through with his slickery, too. But get to the infernal *motive* of the schmuck all them fake Indians was riding for!"

Longarm hauled out the wad of telegrams and handed them over to Pappy Cohen as he said, "I'm almost certain it was a plot to do some serious land grabbing. Nobody traveling with a tent show could have been too interested in prime grazin' or water rights. But at least one of the few serious victims was a squaw-man who found a handy water stop smack between the Tongue River range and the loading pens, here in Sheridan. He was a loner, hardly known to anyone here in town. But Land Management says he did file a homestead claim this very summer. I was hoping the son of a bitch who wanted the Watkins spread would have been dumb enough to file on it as soon as nobody else was living there. But he was too slick or at least he hasn't gotten around to it, yet."

Pappy Cohen, who'd been scanning the yellow telegram Longarm had given him, said, "That squaw-man's layout couldn't have been worth the hiring of a whole Contrary band, even afore it was burnt out, could it?"

"Not alone," Longarm said. "But as you can see if only you'll read on, a mess of claims have been made along the Tongue River. As anyone can see, Little Wolf holds no title to all that prime grazing, summer-long water and cow-sheltering timber. So Interior would be proud to let more civilized looking folk claim it by the full section as rough grazing, if only it wasn't so cluttered up with *Indians*. Only, at the request of the B.I.A. they've been holding off on approving claims, pending some solution to the odd notions of old Little Wolf. The B.I.A. hopes, in time, to either get them Cheyenne to move peaceful to an already established reserve or, failing that, accept an Indian agent and let B.I.A. call that stretch along the Tongue an official retirement home for them proud but weary Cheyenne. Washington doesn't